"What Are You Doing Here, Sam? Why Didn't You Tell Me You're A Sheikh?" Andrea Asked.

Sam pinned her in place with his dark gaze. "Would that have made a difference? Would you have understood what that entailed?"

Sam's voice was mellow and deep and seductively dangerous. But the man reclining against the rear plush leather seat of the limo was a stranger to her now. Andrea couldn't deny he was still beautiful.

"So why did you come back?" Andrea asked.

"Because I couldn't allow another day to pass without seeing you again."

Andrea hated the tiny flutter of her pulse, the glimmer of hope in her heart. "And what did you hope to accomplish after all this time?"

He scrubbed his hand over his jaw. "I need to know if what I have discovered is true."

A stab of fear impaled Andi's chest, making it almost impossible to breathe, to speak. "What would that be?"

"How is our son?"

Bile rose in her throat. Terror closed off her lungs. Protectiveness for her beautiful child pushed it all away. "He's *my* son. Only mine."

Dear Reader,

Get your new year off to a sizzling start by reading six passionate, powerful and provocative new love stories from Silhouette Desire!

Don't miss the exciting launch of DYNASTIES: THE BARONES, the new 12-book continuity series about feuding Italian-American families caught in a web of danger, deceit and desire. Meet Nicholas, the eldest son of Boston's powerful Barone clan, and Gail, the down-to-earth nanny who wins his heart, in *The Playboy & Plain Jane* (#1483) by *USA TODAY* bestselling author Leanne Banks.

In *Beckett's Convenient Bride* (#1484), the final story in Dixie Browning's BECKETT'S FORTUNE miniseries, a detective offers the protection of his home—and loses his heart— to a waitress whose own home is torched after she witnesses a murder. And in *The Sheikh's Bidding* (#1485) by Kristi Gold, an Arabian prince pays dearly to win back his ex-lover and their son.

Reader favorite Sara Orwig completes her STALLION PASS miniseries with *The Rancher, the Baby & the Nanny* (#1486), featuring a daredevil cowboy and the shy miss he hires to care for his baby niece. In *Quade: The Irresistible One* (#1487) by Bronwyn Jameson, sparks fly when two lawyers exchange more than arguments. And great news for all you fans of Harlequin Historicals author Charlene Sands—she's now writing contemporary romances, as well, and debuts in Desire with *The Heart of a Cowboy* (#1488), a reunion romance that puts an ex-rodeo star at close quarters on a ranch with the pregnant widow he's loved silently for years.

Ring in this new year with all six brand-new love stories from Silhouette Desire....

Enjoy!

Joan Marlow Golan

Joan Marlow Golan
Senior Editor, Silhouette Desire

Please address questions and book requests to:
Silhouette Reader Service
U.S.: 3010 Walden Ave., P.O. Box 1325, Buffalo, NY 14269
Canadian: P.O. Box 609, Fort Erie, Ont. L2A 5X3

The Sheikh's Bidding

KRISTI GOLD

Published by Silhouette Books

America's Publisher of Contemporary Romance

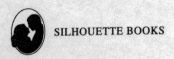

SILHOUETTE BOOKS

ISBN 0-373-76485-5

THE SHEIKH'S BIDDING

Copyright © 2003 by Kristi Goldberg

Visit Silhouette at www.eHarlequin.com

Printed in U.S.A.

KRISTI GOLD

has always believed that love has remarkable healing powers and greatly enjoys writing books featuring romance and commitment. As a bestselling author and Romance Writers of America RITA® Award finalist, she's learned that although accolades are wonderful, the most cherished rewards come from the most unexpected places, namely from stories shared by readers. She welcomes all readers to contact her through her Web site at http://kristigold.com or by mail at P.O. Box 11292, Robinson, TX 76716.

One

"Now, who's going to bid first on this fine little lady?"

Andrea Hamilton shifted nervously on the platform situated in the middle of Winwood Farm's impressive arena, wearing the only dress she owned and a self-conscious smile. Resentful of being called "a fine little lady," she reminded herself that the benefit auction was for a good cause, the reason why she had agreed to donate two months' worth of horse-training services. In turn, she was throwing herself onto the block at the risk of being passed over for someone with more experience.

"Come on, ladies and gentlemen," the auctioneer pleaded. "Give her a chance. She's good."

"At what?" a stumbling drunk in a disheveled tuxedo called from the corner.

Andi shot him a scathing look that he didn't seem to heed, evident from his sickening leer. Now nearing the end of the event, the remaining patrons continued to mill around, paying little attention when the auctioneer called her name again. What if no one even bothered to offer the minimum?

"Five hundred dollars," the drunk called out.

So much for that theory.

"Fifty thousand dollars."

The murmuring crowd was suddenly silenced at the sound of the booming voice delivering the astronomical bid from the back of the arena. Andi froze with her mouth agape, unable to fathom who would make such an offer.

"Fifty-thousand. Going once, going twice! Sold to the gentleman near the door!"

Andi craned her neck to try to see the mystery bidder, but because of her small stature, she only caught a glimpse of the back of a man in traditional Arab dress leaving the building. Royalty, she assumed. Not at all uncommon in racing circles.

Perhaps he had more money than sense. Or it could be that he had questionable intentions. She certainly hoped he understood that he was buying only her training expertise. If he counted on another kind of assistance, he would be sorely disappointed. She had no intention of letting him near her, even if he'd offered fifty million dollars.

With a muttered thank-you directed at the auctioneer, Andi sprinted down the steps as fast as the silly high heels would let her, passed her drink off to a roving waiter and shoved her way through the crowd to the exit at the side of the building. She escaped into the warm Kentucky night, grateful to leave behind the well-heeled racing society, not to mention the drunk. Now she could be on her way home and worry about the phantom bidder tomorrow.

Once she made it to the walkway leading to the front parking lot, an imposing dark-skinned man wearing an equally dark suit blocked her path.

"Miss Hamilton, the sheikh would like to speak with you."

"Excuse me?"

"He is the one who bought your services and he wishes to have a word with you." The man gestured toward a black limousine that spanned a good deal of the nearby curb.

No way, no how, would Andi get into a limo with a stranger even if he was some prince who'd invested a great deal of money to benefit a children's clinic. She rummaged through her purse and pulled out her card. "Here. Have him call me on Monday. We can discuss the terms then."

"He insists that he see you tonight."

Andi's patience scattered in the breeze. "Look, mister, I *insist* I'm not interested in doing that right now. Please tell your boss that I appreciate the gesture and I look forward to meeting him soon." Very far from the truth.

The man looked totally composed, unmovable. "He said that if you give me trouble, I am to present a question."

How weird was this going to get? "What question?"

He averted his gaze for a moment, the only hint of

discomfort in his staid expression. "He asks do you still hang your dreams on the stars?"

Andi's heart vaulted into her throat and rapidly fluttered in a frightening rhythm. Haunting memories whirled her back to a time seven years before. Memories of lying in a field of grass beneath a predawn sky, alone, immersed in tears until he had come to her. Memories of a sensual awakening that had begun with tragedy and ended with bittersweet bliss. One special moment, one unforgettable man.

One true love.

Why hang your dreams on the stars, Andrea? Why not something more tangible?

His voice came back to her then, mellow and deep and seductively dangerous. That night in her grief she had turned to him, only to be left behind, left alone except for one precious gift that served to remind her every day what she could never have.

Andi trembled and chafed her palms down her arms, suddenly chilled. "And this man's name?" she asked, although she feared she already knew the answer.

"Sheikh Samir Yaman."

Andi had known him only as Sam, known only of his family's wealth, not his title. He'd been her big brother's best friend who'd spent the better part of his college days at their home as an adopted member of the family. She'd been a teenager smitten by an "older" exotic man who had teased her mercilessly, saw her only as Paul's kid sister, until that night a few weeks after she'd turned eighteen when unforeseen tragedy had created new life. Ironically, only hours before, another life had been taken away.

But that was ages ago, water under the proverbial bridge, and she didn't want to unearth the pain or face him again, knowing she ran a great risk by doing so, both to her heart and the secret she had hidden from him for years.

The man walked to the limo's door and opened it wide. "Miss Hamilton?"

"I don't—"

"Get in, Andrea."

The deep timbre of the magnetic voice drew her forward against her will. She suddenly found herself sliding into the limo as if she had no control over her body or mind. How familiar that concept. From the moment she'd met him, he'd held her captive with his charms, his easy manner, his air of mystery, eventually his touch.

The door closed and a small light snapped on, revealing a man reclining against the rear plush, leather seat facing Andi. A man who was anything but a stranger to her—at least he hadn't been at one time in her life. She stared at him for a long moment, her heart creating a furious cadence in her chest as if it wanted to escape as badly as she did. Yet she couldn't move, couldn't speak when her gaze made contact with his intense eyes.

He raked the kaffiyeh from his head as if to prove he was the man she'd known all those years ago. But he wasn't quite the same. The changes were subtle, no doubt brought about by maturity, yet she couldn't deny he was still beautiful, with the same thick, dark hair that curled at his nape, same masculine jaw, same wonderful mouth now framed by a shading of evening whiskers. Although his near-black eyes held the familiar elusiveness, they also looked weary, not bright and youthful as before. She imagined hers mirrored that disillusionment, only now they more than likely revealed her shock.

Andi struggled to stay strong in his presence. "What are you doing here, Sam?"

His high-impact smile appeared, gleaming white against his caramel-colored skin, revealing the single dimple creasing his left cheek. Yet he seemed to be fighting the smile as much as Andi was fighting her reaction to it. "It's been a while since anyone has called me that." He gestured toward the small built-in bar to his left. "Would you like something to drink, Andrea?"

Something to drink? He expected to waltz back into her life after all these years and ply her with pleasantries?

Andi welcomed the force of her sudden anger, the anchor it provided against the sea of emotions. "No, I don't want a drink. I want to know why you're here. I haven't heard a word from you since Paul's funeral. Not one word."

He shifted in his seat and glanced away. "That was necessary, Andrea. I had obligations to fulfill in my country."

And none to her, Andi decided. "Why didn't you tell me you're a sheikh?"

He pinned her in place with his dark gaze. "Would that have made a difference? Would you have understood what that entailed?"

Probably not. It also didn't change the fact that he'd disappeared without any explanation. Regardless of his status, she was hard-pressed to understand a concept as foreign to her as the clothes he now wore. "So why did you come back?"

"Because I couldn't allow another day to pass without seeing you again."

Andi hated the tiny flutter of her pulse, the glimmer of hope in her heart. "Well, that's great. What did you hope to accomplish after all this time?"

He slipped out of his robes, the final garment that distinguished ordinary man from revered royalty, and tossed them aside, leaving him dressed in a white tailored shirt and black slacks. Try as she might, Andi couldn't help but notice the breadth of his chest and the spattering of dark hair revealed at his open collar. In a matter of years he had gone from a boyishly handsome college student to a devastatingly gorgeous man. And she would be smart to ignore those differences, the heat coursing through her traitorous body.

He scrubbed a hand over his jaw. "I need to know if what I have discovered is true."

A stab of fear impaled Andi's chest, making it almost impossible to breathe, to speak. "What would that be?"

He leveled his serious eyes on her. "I know that you've struggled with the farm, barely managing to get by. Several times over the years I've considered offering my help financially but decided you would have too much pride to accept."

Relief replaced the fear. Maybe he didn't know everything. "You are so right about that. I don't need your help, financially or otherwise."

"Are you certain about that, Andrea?"

"Positive. I'm doing fine."

"But you've never married."

"I'm not interested in finding a husband," she said, when in reality no one had ever come close to being Samir Yaman's equal. No one had ever affected her in the same way, with the same magic. She'd told herself time and again those were the fantasies of a young girl and they shouldn't exist now that she was a woman. Yet no matter how hard she'd tried to convince herself to forget him, forget what it had felt like to be in his arms, it hadn't worked. No man had ever measured up. No man probably ever would. Seeing Sam again brought home that painful truth. Knowing who he was, what he was, only cemented the certainty that she could never be a part of his world.

"I have another question for you," he said quietly.

She was afraid of his questions, afraid of the hold he still seemed to have on her. "If this has to do with the past, I don't want to go there. It's over."

"It's not over, Andrea, no matter how much you wish it to be." His voice, his expression, balanced on the edge of anger as he locked on to her eyes. She couldn't look away even though she wanted to. "How is your son?"

The fear advanced once again. "How do you know about him?"

"I have the means to learn anything I wish about anyone."

Damn his arrogance, his sudden appearance that could very well destroy her world once again. "My son is fine, thank you."

"And his father?"

Bile rose in her throat. Terror closed off her lungs. Protectiveness for her beautiful child pushed it all away. "He's *my* son. Only mine."

"He has to have a father, Andrea."

"No, he doesn't. His father isn't in the picture. He never has been."

"Then he is mine, isn't he?"

Oh, heavens, what was she going to do now? Had he returned to claim his child? She wouldn't let him, not without a fight. "Believe what you will. This conversation is finished."

"It is far from finished."

"What do you want from me?"

"I want to know why you never told me about him."

She released a mirthless laugh to veil her anxiety. "How would I have done that? You disappeared with no number to call, no way to get in touch with you."

"Then you admit I am his father?"

"I'm admitting nothing. I'm saying it doesn't matter, *Sheikh* Yaman. None of this matters. The past is over. I don't want to dredge it up again."

"It doesn't matter what either of us wants, Andrea. What matters is our child. I'm determined to settle this. If not now, then later. And soon."

Andi opened the door and tried to slide out, but not before he caught her hand and said, "I will be in touch."

She responded with tingles where his fingers curled around hers, with regret when she saw a sadness in his expression that she'd only seen one other time. But that surprising display of vulnerability soon disappeared, and his eyes once again took on the mystery—deep, dark waters that threatened to suck Andi into their shadowy depths. Without breaking his gaze, he turned her hand over and slid a slow fingertip

along her palm, reminding Andi of that long-ago
night when his masterful touch had made her beg him
to stop, beg him to never stop.

Andi yanked her hand from his grasp and hurried
away to her truck, sprinted as fast as her heels would
let her. She raced from the panic that he might intend
to take her child away from her, ran from the love
for him that had never died.

But in her heart she knew that no matter how hard
she tried to get away, Andrea Hamilton could never
escape Sam Yaman, even after he left her again.

Samir Yaman sat alone in darkness in the hotel
suite, surrounded by the luxury he had known most
of his life. He needed a drink and would welcome the
bitter taste of whiskey on his tongue, but he didn't
dare give in to the craving, not when he needed a
clear head. Truthfully, he hadn't touched alcohol
since that night—the night he had made two grave
mistakes.

After all this time Sam had not been able to escape
the guilt over his best friend's demise. He had realized all too late that he should have stopped Paul's
postgraduation drinking binge, but he'd allowed him
his freedom that night, feeling it had been hard-earned
due to the responsibility placed upon Paul after his
father's death. That freedom had cost Paul his life,
and Sam still paid the price for his own poor judgment.

And if only he hadn't gone to Andrea after he'd
left the hospital with the knowledge that her brother
had not survived. If only he had waited until dawn
instead of following her to the pond where she always

went to think, that night to mourn. If only he hadn't forgotten that she was no more than a grief-stricken girl who had needed comfort. Giving in to that need had been his second mistake. He'd been powerless to resist her, perhaps because of his own need to forget or perhaps because she had always been his ultimate weakness.

She still was.

He had recognized that tonight the moment he'd glimpsed her standing before the masses, wearing a black dress that revealed a woman's curves. She had looked poised and proud until no one offered a decent bid—the reason he had spontaneously decided to remedy that situation.

Leaning his head back, Sam closed his eyes against images of Andrea that burned in his mind, a flame that would not die, had not died since he'd left her the day they had buried her brother, his friend. No matter how he tried, they refused to disappear, forcing him to acknowledge what he had known all along—time and distance had changed nothing.

Her eyes were still azure, her long hair still the color of a desert sunset, reds mixed with gold. He imagined she still possessed a free spirit, an undeniable passion for life, a strong heart, the attributes that had attracted him to her from the beginning. Qualities he still admired. Yet he had sensed defiance when she'd entered the car, perhaps even hatred. He couldn't blame her. She had much to hate about him. At times he hated himself. He had thrust himself into his duty, losing his honor in the process by not facing his failures.

Since his return to Barak, he'd had his guard and

confidant, Rashid, covertly track Andrea's life as much as possible. But a few months ago, when he had planned the trip to the States, Rashid had finally revealed that Andrea had a six-year-old son. No matter what Andrea had told him tonight, Sam knew the boy was his. The timing was too coincidental for it not to be the case. He intended to prove it and make certain the child's needs were being met, though he could never claim him, or Andrea.

He could promise Andrea nothing beyond providing for her and their child. He could never tell her all the things he felt as a man. He could never speak of the times he had considered giving up his wealth, his legacy, to be with her again. She would never know that not one day had passed when he hadn't thought of her, longed for her.

Sheikh Samir Yaman, first son of the ruler of Barak, heir to his father's legacy, was bound by duty to his family, his country, groomed from birth to lead, and tied to an arrangement of marriage to a woman he had never touched. A woman he would never love, for his heart always had, always would, belong to a woman he could not have—Andrea Hamilton.

"Mama! There's a big black car in the driveway!"

Andi froze with her arms full of the clothes she'd gathered for her son's summer trip to camp. She had hoped this wouldn't happen today. Hoped that Sam would have waited to contact her until tomorrow. If only she'd hurried and gotten Chance out of the house sooner, she might have been able to avoid this scene. Maybe she still could.

"Get away from the window, Chance."

He looked back over his shoulder, confusion calling out from dark eyes much like his father's. "Why, Mama?"

"Because it's not nice to stare at strangers, that's why."

Ignoring her, Chance continued to look out the window. "He's got a towel on his head and a big man with him."

"Chance Samuel Paul Hamilton, come over here right now and help me get your things together, otherwise you'll miss the bus."

With a sigh he turned and trudged toward her. "I just want to look at the man."

That's the last thing Andi wanted, at least now. She would prefer to put Sam off until she could get her child on his way to camp. Then she would deal with the questions that were sure to come—or demands as the case might be.

Andi stuffed the clothing into the nylon tote and told Chance, "Get your toothbrush and put it in the plastic bag in the bathroom with your medicine. Then pick out some books and make sure you pack your paper so you can write home."

Chance's lip pooched out in a pout. "Then can I meet him?"

"Not today. I'm not sure what he wants." A less-than-truthful version. Andi knew exactly what he wanted, to see his son. "He'll probably be gone before you're finished packing."

"I'll hurry up." With that, Chance sprinted into the hall.

Andi was right behind him, relieved that he'd gone toward the hall bathroom, not down the stairs. Her son was well behaved most of the time, although he could be determined. He came by it naturally, she guessed, considering she was much the same way. That had gotten her into trouble on more than one occasion. A particular summer night came to mind.

The doorbell sounded, jarring Andi into action. "I'll get it," came from the first floor.

"I'll get it, Tess," she called to her aunt in hopes of stopping her. "I—"

"Well good gracious! Sam!"

Too late. Andi should have forewarned Tess that they might be having a visitor, and exactly who that visitor would be.

Andi slowly walked down the stairs that ended in the entryway now containing her aunt, a bodyguard and her son's father. Sam immediately looked up and met her gaze. She hugged her arms across her middle as she spanned the remaining stairs. When she came to the last one, she was afraid to go any farther, especially when Sam kept staring at her as if he could see all the secrets she had held in her heart for years.

Tess turned a huge grin on Andi. "Well, looky here what the cat dragged in, Andi. It's our Sam."

Our Sam. How odd that sounded at the moment. That's exactly what they'd called him years ago. But he wasn't Andi's. Beyond that one night he never had been, nor would he ever be.

Andi managed a fake smile and spoke through clenched teeth. "I thought you would call first."

"And give you fair warning?" he said with a cynical grin.

"What's this get-up you're wearing?" Tess asked with a one-handed sweep toward Sam's robes.

He finally took his attention away from Andi, allowing her to release her breath. "My straitjacket, I'm afraid."

"You don't look crazy," Tess said. "You look like a break in the clouds after the rain. Now come here and give me a hug."

Sam complied, lifting Tess off her feet as he had so many times before. After setting her down, he asked, "You don't happen to have any of your famous coffee on to brew, do you?"

Tess favored him with a sunny smile. "You know I always keep a pot on. Come into the kitchen and sit a spell."

The bodyguard remained positioned at the door while Andi followed Tess and Sam into the breakfast room. Once there, Tess poured him a cup of coffee and said, "I'm going to run upstairs and check on the boy. You two have a nice visit." She hurried away, leaving Andi alone to face her past.

Sam took the chair with its back to the bay window, the place he'd always sat during family dinners. Andi refused to sit, resenting the fact that Sam had made himself comfortable as if he planned to stay awhile. Except for his clothing, he even looked comfortable, at home, as if he'd never left. But he had left, and Andi couldn't believe that Tess had acted as if he'd only been gone for a week or so, as if nothing had changed. When in fact everything had changed. But Tess had always loved Sam just the way she loved Andi and Paul. Just the way she loved Chance.

"Mama?"

Andi's gaze shot to the doorway leading to the hall where her son now stood, his large brown eyes focused on the man he considered a fascinating stranger. Tess was nowhere to be seen, leading Andi to believe that her aunt had a hand in this spontaneous introduction of father and son.

Andi didn't know what to do, what to say. But if she didn't act normal, Chance would immediately sense something was wrong, and she didn't want to frighten him.

She held out her hand to him. "Come here, sweetie."

When Chance walked forward and stood in front of her, Andi braced her palms on his frail shoulders. "Honey, this is Mr. Yaman."

Sam rose, and Andi immediately noticed the wonder in his eyes, the undeniable emotion as he looked upon his child. With his thick dark hair, his coffee-colored eyes, Chance was almost the mirror image of his father. There was no longer any use in denying the truth.

"I'm Samir," he finally said, his smile now aimed at his child, not Andi. "You may call me Sam."

Chance's mouth opened in surprise. "That's kind of like my name, the Sam part, anyway. Chance Samuel Paul Hamilton. Aunt Tess sometimes calls me Little Bit." He sounded as if that was totally distasteful.

"You have a good strong name." Sam sent only a cursory glance in Andi's direction before turning his attention back to his son, but not before she saw another glimpse of regret and sadness. He was probably thinking about Paul, maybe even thinking about how much he'd missed in Chance's life. Andi couldn't let that sway her. She had to stay strong for her child's sake.

Tess suddenly reappeared into the kitchen. "Don't be scared, Little Bit. Shake the man's hand. He's an old friend."

Chance looked back at Andi, and she nodded her approval, then he moved forward and took the hand his father offered. Sam's smile revealed his pride. Andi couldn't blame him. She had felt that way about her child from the moment he was born.

After a hearty, exaggerated shake, Chance asked, "What's that on your head?"

"It's a kaffiyeh," Sam said.

"What's it for?"

"It's part of my official dress. I come from a country far away. I am a sheikh."

"Well, I'll be durned," Tess muttered.

Chance still looked confused. "A sheet?"

"A prince," Andi stated, grateful that Sam had enough wherewithal not to announce he was her son's father.

Chance glanced back at her. "Like *The Little Prince?*"

Andi smiled over the reference to one of his favorite books. "More like *Aladdin.*"

"Oh." He stared at Sam a moment longer. "Do you have a flying carpet?"

Sam laughed then, a low rich laugh that brought back more of Andi's cherished memories. "I'm afraid I have no magic carpet."

"Just a big black car," Chance said, sounding awed over that fact.

Andi took Chance's hand, determined to usher him out before he asked more questions. "Honey, it's time to go to camp. If we don't leave, you'll miss your bus.''

Amazingly, Chance looked disappointed over leaving his newfound friend. He'd been bugging her for weeks, counting the days until his first trip to camp, something Andi had been dreading even though she knew it would be good for him. Now he looked as if he couldn't care less. "Can I stay and talk to the prince a little longer?"

"How long will you be away at this camp?" Sam asked.

"Two weeks," Andi answered for her son. "I'm sure you'll be gone—"

"I promise I will be here when you return," Sam said, his eyes still leveled on his child.

Chance's grin widened, revealing the left-sided dimple that served as another reminder of his parentage. "Can I ride in your car when I get home?"

"Most certainly."

Andi gave Chance a nudge toward the door. "Let's go."

"Andrea," Sam said from behind her. "One other thing."

She looked back to find that Tess had taken a chair across from Sam who had seated himself once again, his hands folded before him, looking much too cozy for Andi's comfort.

"What other thing?" she asked, although she wasn't certain she really wanted to know.

"I will be here when you return."

Exactly what Andi had longed for through many yesterdays, and what she greatly feared today.

Two

He had viewed the many ruins in Rome, Sacré Coeur at Montmartre in Paris, the Acropolis in Athens. Yet those experiences had paled in comparison to gazing upon his child for the first time.

Now Sam could only sit in silence, holding fast to the wish that he could recapture the years and experience every one of his son's milestones. But that was not possible, and not enough hours existed to make up for lost time.

"Are you okay, Sam?"

He looked up from his untouched coffee and met Tess's compassionate, gray eyes. "As well as can be expected."

"I guess finding out about the boy kind of shocked you."

"I knew about him before I arrived."

Tess's eyes widened. "You knew?"

"Did Andrea not tell you that we spoke last night following the auction?"

"Heck no, she didn't tell me that. She only told me that some guy paid a truckload of money for her to train his horse."

"I was the one. A small price to pay for the opportunity to know my child." And the opportunity to once again be in Andrea's presence, if only for a while. Perhaps he was somehow torturing himself, knowing he could never touch her, never hold her or make love to her again. Some things had not changed with the passage of time.

"How long have you known?" Tess asked.

"I found out a few months ago, when I knew I would be returning. I had someone investigate Andrea's whereabouts. I didn't know for certain that he was mine until I spoke with her last evening."

"She admitted you're his father?"

"No, but I surmised that fact because of his age and some of what she said to me. I had no doubts after I saw him." Sam pushed the cup aside and leaned back. "How long have you known?"

Tess propped her cheek on her palm and sighed. "I knew something was wrong with Andi after Paul's death, something more than losing her brother. I finally nagged her enough until she told me she was pregnant. The girl tried to convince me she'd been with some boy in town, but when Chance was born, that's when I knew for sure he was yours."

The guilt fisted in Sam's belly and held on tightly. "It was the night Paul died, Tess. We turned to each other for comfort. Never before Andrea had I been so careless. I know that doesn't relieve me of the responsibility, but I want you to know that I never intended it to happen."

"I know you didn't. I also know that Andi had her sights set on you the minute you walked through the front door that first time. Add that to her mourning Paul's death, it's not surprising at all."

"That does not excuse my behavior, my failure to protect her," Sam said adamantly. "I should never have allowed it to happen."

Tess leaned forward and laid a hand on his arm. "It's too late to worry about the what-I-should-have-dones. Question is, what are you going to do now?"

Sam knew what he wanted to do. He also knew what he could not do. He couldn't get involved with Andrea again knowing what he faced on his return home. He also could not abandon his child. "I would like to take the month I have here in the States to get to know my son."

Tess frowned. "So you're gonna try to cram six years into a few weeks?"

"I suppose I am. I also want to set up a trust fund to make sure that his needs are met."

Tess glared at him. "Let's get one thing straight, Mr. Sheikh. Andi has worked like the devil to meet that boy's needs. After the life insurance money ran out last year, she broke horses no one else wanted to break, all at the risk of getting herself hurt, or worse, just to pay the bills and put food on the table. I've done my part, too, and you can bet Chance has been happy, except for the diabetes."

Searing panic rushed through Sam. "Diabetes?"

"Yeah. Guess Andi didn't bother to tell you that,

either. The camp he's going to is a summer program for diabetic kids. It almost killed Andi to let him go, but she decided it would do him a world of good.''

"How long has he had this diabetes?"

"He was diagnosed a little over a year ago. But he's doing okay after having a few setbacks. He's a regular little trooper, I tell you.''

Sam experienced an overwhelming pain for his child, the need to take that pain away, if only he could. "If I had known, I would have done more. I would have sent him to the finest doctors, the best hospitals.''

"And it wouldn't have changed a thing, Sam. He's stuck with this disease, and we can only hope and pray that someday they'll find a cure. In the meantime, we plan to treat him like a normal kid. Or at least I try to do that. Andi's pretty protective.''

That much he'd witnessed earlier. "With my money, she can have more financial freedom.''

"She won't take your money.''

"She won't refuse as long as she knows I have our son's best interest at heart.''

"Maybe, but you hurt her pretty badly by just running off and not staying in touch. I'm not sure how you're going to deal with that.''

Neither did Sam, but he had to try. "After we've had the opportunity to talk further, I hope we can come to an understanding.''

She stared at the cup a few more moments before looking up once again. "Okay, so you want to spend some time with Chance, and I think that's a good idea, which means you need to be close by. So the way I see it, you'll need to move in here with us.''

Sam secretly admitted he had thought about that, living once again in the place he had considered his true home in America, but he could only imagine Andrea's reaction. "I doubt your niece will agree to that plan."

"Let me handle her. I suggest that you get in that limo and hightail it out of here to go and get your things. She won't be back for another hour or so, since she's got to stop by the feed store. That should give you enough time to settle in. You can have my room. I'll stay in the bunkhouse."

"With Mr. Parker?"

Tess patted her short, gray hair and glanced away. "No. Riley's working for someone else because Andi couldn't afford to keep him on. He still stops by now and then."

Sam grinned when color rose to Tess's careworn face. "He has yet to propose marriage?"

"He has, every day, but I'm too old to consider getting married."

"But not too old to…?" Sam let his words trail off on a question, unable to resist teasing her a bit.

"Too old for a good old-fashioned tumble? No one's too old for that, Sam. Not when it comes to someone you care about."

Images filtered into Sam's consciousness, visions of making love to Andrea, seeing satisfaction in her eyes, not sadness or hatred. But he could not consider something so foolish again, no matter how much he ached to do that very thing.

"Perhaps I should wait until Chance returns from camp," he said, thinking that might be favorable to being alone in the house with Andrea.

Tess shrugged. "You could, but I figure while you're here, you could earn your keep. The place is falling down around our ears, especially the barn. Might be nice if you could help fix the place up a bit. You could take the time to do that before Chance gets back."

At least that would occupy his hands during the day. But during the night... "I would be happy to do that. I must admit, I've missed engaging in manual labor since I've been away."

She sent him another questioning look. "You know, I'm surprised some girl hasn't snatched you up."

Sam mentally winced. "I am to be married by the end of summer."

"Does Andi know about this?" Tess did well to keep the shock from her expression, but it resounded in her tone.

"No. I prefer not to speak about it."

Tess stood and went to the counter to refill her coffee. "I guess you know what you're doing."

He knew exactly what he was doing—entering into a union with a woman for whom he felt nothing, an alliance that would benefit both their families. A life that held little promise of satisfaction all in the name of producing an heir with royal blood. "I have no choice in the matter."

Tess carried her cup back to the table and re-claimed her seat, staring at him intensely. "You're wrong, Sam. Life is about choices. Can you live with this one?"

Before he had returned to Andrea, he had come to

accept his fate. Now that he had seen her again, he wasn't as certain as before.

He could not consider that now. First and foremost, he had to consider his child's well-being, to make memories that would last a lifetime. And in order to have that opportunity, he must convince Andrea to trust him again.

Andi didn't trust Sam or his motives. Worse, she didn't trust herself around him. Today she had cried more than a few tears seeing her son off for the first time. She wasn't sure she had enough strength to deal with his father. But she had to deal with him. Chance's welfare was of the utmost importance, and she intended to find out what Sam had planned in that regard.

Pulling up behind the limo, she put the truck in Park and slid out, bolstering her courage. The bodyguard was seated on the front porch glider, looking serious, his arms folded across his chest. When Andi approached, he stood.

She stuck out her hand for a formal introduction. "I didn't catch your name."

He glanced at her hand then reluctantly took it for a brief shake. "Mr. Rashid."

"Nice to meet you, Mr. Rashid. You're welcome in the house, you know."

"It is best I remain here to allow you and the sheikh some privacy."

Andi shrugged. "Suit yourself, but I'm sure this won't take long."

Rashid executed a slight bow. "As you say, Miss Hamilton."

Andi yanked open the door, prepared to face whatever might come, yet she couldn't have prepared for Sam sitting on the living room sofa, dressed in casual slacks and knit shirt, his dark head bent as he thumbed through a photo album containing pictures of Chance from birth to the present day. So engrossed was he in the task, he didn't bother to look up. His preoccupation gave Andi a chance to study him while he journeyed through the pictorial history of their child.

Leaning back, he propped the album on one crossed leg and smiled. His smile faded and his expression turned melancholy, wistful. Andi closed her eyes and willed away the threatening emotions, the regrets.

Once she felt more composed, she approached the sofa. "He was such a beautiful baby."

Startled, Sam looked up and erased the tenderness from his features, but it didn't quite leave his eyes. "Yes, he was."

Andi joined him on the sofa, leaving as much distance between them as she could and still be able to view the pictures with Sam. How many times had she dreamed of this? How many times had she hoped that one day he would return? More times than she could count. And now that the moment had arrived, she wasn't sure how to handle it.

"What made you decide to call him Chance?" Sam asked.

"Other than I like the name, I guess you could say he was my chance to have someone who loved me without conditions." Her chance to have part of Sam that she could have with her always, but she wouldn't admit that to him.

She pointed to the photo of Chance on his first birthday, a mound of icing on top of his dark head. "He really tore into that cake. He wore more than he ate."

He turned the page to a picture of Chance on a pony. "I see that he has inherited his mother's love of horses."

"Yes. That's Scamp. She's still with us although I'm not sure for how long. She's about twenty years old now. I don't know what he'll do when we lose her."

"I'll buy him another."

"Some things can't be easily replaced."

He kept his attention focused on the photograph. "I have learned that to be a strong truth."

Now seemed like a good time to tell him her greatest concern. "I can't let you take him from me, Sam."

He closed the album, slipped it onto the coffee table and leaned forward, hands clasped between his parted knees, but he failed to look directly at her. "Is that what you think I've come to do, take him away from you?"

"Is it?"

"No, Andrea. He belongs here with you."

Although he sounded certain, doubts still hounded Andi. "So now that you've seen him, you're going to turn your back and walk away?"

He pinned her with his fiery dark eyes, his expression hard, angry. "I have no intention of turning my back on him. I will set up a bank account in your name to pay for his expenses. As I understand it, his medical bills have been a burden on you, according to Tess.''

Damn Tess. "He's doing okay, and I'm managing to pay the bills a little at a time. So it's really not necessary for you to give us any money.''

His features softened. "I insist that you let me do this for him. For you.''

"I'll think about it.'' And she would, but not for herself. After all, Sam did have an obligation to their son, and she could use the extra money for his expenses. Not to mention, the sheikh probably had several fortunes to spare. Because of Chance, she would put away her pride and allow him to help.

Sam walked to the shelf across the room and ran a fingertip along the edge of the frame that held the most recent picture of Chance, as if trying to connect to the child he'd only known for a few hours. "Do they know why he has this diabetes?''

"No. It just happened. It's not anyone's fault.''

He glanced back. "And he's doing well?''

"Most of the time, now that we have his insulin and diet regulated. He's so brave. He doesn't even complain when he has to have his shots.''

"I hate that he has suffered." Turning his attention back to the photo, he released a long sigh. "Has he asked about me?''

Andi rose and stood behind him. "Yes, several times in the past few years.''

"And what did you tell him?''

"I told him that you couldn't stay, that you lived far away in another land. I told him that you loved him and you'd be with us if you could.''

Slowly Sam faced her. "Then you did not lie to him."

"I don't know. Did I?"

He lowered his head. "It's true. I couldn't stay in America, Andrea. And now that I have seen him, I know that I would die before I let any harm come to him."

Andi swallowed hard around the lump in her throat. "I'm glad you feel that way, but I'm also worried about what we should tell him."

Sam raised his dark eyes to her. "I will leave that up to you, but I would like for him to know that I'm his father."

In a perfect world Andi would consider that to be a good idea. But this wasn't a perfect situation by any means. "Then what? 'Hey, Chance, I'm your dad and I'm sorry about this, but I have to go back and do my princely duties'?"

"I can return to visit during the summers when he's not in school."

"Is that enough, Sam? Will that ever be enough for him?"

He streaked a hand over his nape and sighed. "Would you have given up the opportunity to have spent time with Paul and your father even knowing they would be taken from you?"

Andi cursed his logic. "No, I wouldn't take anything for that time with them. But that's different. You'd be absent by choice, not death."

"Sometimes choices are made for us."

"You mean your duty? I'm not sure he'd understand why your position takes precedence over him. In time he might come to resent you."

"As his mother does?" Sam asked in a low, steady voice.

Andi had to admit that she'd resented his sudden departure. Resented that he had made love to her, created a child then left her alone to raise their son, left her alone to deal with her grief over her brother's death. But she couldn't fault him, at least when it came to Chance, since he hadn't known about him until now. He also hadn't made that possible because of his loyalty to a way of life that Andi couldn't even begin to understand. Worse, he hadn't even tried to explain or to stay in touch.

Still, she had to do what was best for everyone, even if that included calling a truce.

"I'm past my resentment, Sam."

"But you'll never forgive me, will you?"

"I have forgiven you." To a point, but she would never be able to forget.

His eyes took on the cast of satisfaction. "I'm pleased by that, Andrea. I only hope that I can earn your trust."

That would be a bit harder, in Andrea's opinion. She still feared that Sam might change his mind and try to take her son back to his country, especially after he got to know him. Yet she was willing to give him the benefit of the doubt, at least for the time being. "So where are you staying?"

"Here."

"I beg your pardon?"

"Tess told me it would be best if I remain nearby, and I agree. She wishes to reside in the bunkhouse during my stay, though I argued against it. But she insisted. I've brought a few of my things and I'll send

Rashid back to the hotel in Lexington to wait for me until I'm ready to leave.''

Andi fought the bite of apprehension. If Sam stayed under the same roof, she couldn't avoid seeing him on a daily basis. And with their son away at camp for two weeks, she worried that she might not be able to resist him. "I think you should wait until Chance returns before you move in.''

"I have promised Tess I will help do some repairs while I'm here, before Chance comes back.''

Tess. Always thinking of everything, darn it. "I guess I could use the help,'' Andi admitted. She could also use some courage. Right now it was all she could do not to reach out and touch him, send her fingertips over the fine lines framing his mouth, his incredible lips that now formed a grim line as he studied her. Be brave, she told herself.

As if he intended to test her nerve, Sam took her hand into his, creating pleasant warmth that flowed through her whole body. One simple touch, and already she was battling for control. But she had to remain in control, prove to herself, and to him, that she was much stronger than before. Prove that her memories were colored by the fantasies of a young girl, dreams that no longer existed in a woman's reality. She intended to conduct her own test.

Putting her best smile forward, she pulled her hand from his grasp and opened her arms. "Welcome home, Sam.''

His gaze roved over her from head to toe in a long, lingering look of appreciation, then finally he accepted her embrace. He felt good against her, strong and solid and warm. She remembered how wonderful it had been to hold him close, remembered his exotic scent, his overwhelming heat. Remembered how she had missed having him in her life, left only with her hopes of his return and memories of one night when he had been completely hers.

Trembling with the force of her reaction, she pulled out of his arms and stepped back. Her greatest fear was now realized.

Nothing had really changed, even after all these years.

Sam brushed a tender kiss across her cheek and studied her with those damnable mysterious eyes, dark and intense and capable of bringing her to her knees.

"Thank you, Andrea. It's good to be home."

If only it was home, Sam thought as he stood in the middle of the aged barn. He had chosen to come to the stable first, his favorite place. A place where he had spent many an hour with Paul and Andrea, assisting with the daily chores, shoveling manure, unloading feed, watering the remaining two horses that had belonged to Paul and Andrea's father before his death, and any others that had happened upon the premises, thanks to a young woman who couldn't say no.

Even then, Andrea would bring home someone's colt or filly to break, most of the time solely for the thrill of it, not for the pay. Today, out of the dozen or so stalls, only four were occupied, one by Chance's pony.

This would never do, Sam decided. He needed to help Andrea acquire some horses to train immediately. Most of those he owned belonged to a syndicate, but that did not mean he couldn't purchase one that belonged solely to him. He had a gift for choosing good prospects, the reason why he had come to Kentucky to attend the sales. In fact, he had been approached at the auction regarding a promising two-year-old filly. One phone call and the mare would be his, though she was priced at half a million U.S. dollars. That didn't matter. After all, he had paid for Andrea's training expertise; he might as well put that investment to good use. But first he must repair a few stalls.

After rummaging through the tack room for a hammer and nails, Sam set out to make the barn more serviceable. Unfortunately, he pounded his thumb on more than one occasion, yet he welcomed the pain. For seven years he had done nothing more than paperwork, since manual labor was considered demeaning for royalty. But Sam was in America now, in a barn, not Barak, therefore he could labor to his heart's delight.

"What on earth are you doing?"

He turned toward the entry to find Andrea staring at him as if he had grown fangs. He had no fangs, only two nails in his mouth. He spoke around them. "I'm repairing these stalls before an injury occurs." Considering his deplorable skills, an injury could very well occur. To him.

She took a few steps forward and braced her hands on her hips. "In case you haven't noticed, there isn't a horse in that stall, and I doubt there's going to be one anytime soon."

Turning away from her, he removed the nails from

his mouth and hammered one into the wooden slat. "You're wrong, Andrea."

"What are you talking about?"

He faced her again and swiped the sweat from his brow with a forearm. "I've recently purchased a filly." Or he would by day's end. "If you recall, I bid an obscene amount of money for your services, and I expect to collect."

At the moment he would like to collect on several things, none having to do with her training skills. He couldn't seem to pull his gaze away from the ragged white T-shirt she now wore or the faded jeans that adhered to the bow of her hips like a second skin. His body stirred, calling attention to a need that had been denied far too long. Reminding him that Andrea could still affect him without attempting to do so.

She strolled to his side and leaned a shoulder against the stall, facing him. "You mean to tell me that you actually intend for me to train your horse."

"That's precisely what I'm telling you." He should be telling her that, if she knew what was best for her, for them both, from this point forward she would wear a bra.

She frowned. "And when is this horse supposed to be here?"

"I will arrange for her to arrive in two days. That should give me time to repair the stall."

Andrea smiled, amusement dancing in her blue eyes. "You intend to do this in your good clothes?"

Sam looked down at his slacks and shirt, then back up again. "I'm afraid this is all I have at the present. I'll go into town and buy something suitable tomorrow."

"Can't you have Mr. Rashid do it for you?"

"I've sent him back to the hotel to field calls. I prefer that no one knows where I am." Then perhaps he could avoid his father's questions.

"You don't need his protection?"

Only from his desire for Andrea, and he doubted Rashid could aid him in that regard. "I am relatively safe at the moment." Yet still in danger of losing his control in her presence.

"You really don't have to buy anything, at least not today," she said. "I'm sure I can find you something to wear."

He let his eyes travel down the length of her—very much at his own peril when he noticed her nipples had hardened beneath the thin shirt. "I doubt that I will fit into your jeans."

She crossed her arms over her chest, much to his disappointment and relief. "Not mine. Yours. You left some jeans here. They're in the cedar chest in the attic."

"And they are still intact?"

"I'm sure they are. Of course, there could be one major problem. You were much skinnier then."

"Skinnier?"

She sent a long glance down his body, much the same as he had hers. "Yep. You've filled out quite a bit."

He was definitely filling out in some very obvious places. To avoid embarrassment, he turned back to the stall and surveyed his handiwork. "Give me a moment and we can go to the attic."

"Why can't we go now?" she asked, sounding confused.

Obviously she was still somewhat naive. He took in a deep draw of air but refused to turn around. "As soon as I'm finished with this board, I will join you. At the moment I prefer not to stop what I'm doing."

He, as well, preferred to stop his craving for her, but he doubted that would happen soon—if ever.

Three

Sitting cross-legged on the attic floor, Andi pulled the jeans from the cedar chest where she'd kept them along with other special mementos—Chance's baby clothes, his first shoes, a few of Paul's things, treasures that she couldn't bear to part with. She fought back more tears, already missing her son and he'd only been gone a few hours. Admittedly, already missing Sam even though he wouldn't leave again for several weeks.

She set the jeans aside and rummaged through the pile in the chest, coming upon Paul's high school football jersey sporting the number seven. Lucky seven, Paul had said. If only his luck had held out, before he'd been ripped from her life, never having children of his own, never knowing Chance.

How Paul would have loved his nephew, loved

playing uncle. If he hadn't died, maybe things would have been different. She probably wouldn't have made love with Sam. And she wouldn't have Chance.

She couldn't imagine not having her son in her life. She also couldn't turn back time and she couldn't keep wondering about what might have been. Even if Paul had survived, Sam would have returned to his country, his duty. Hadn't he all but admitted that to her?

Dropping the jersey back into the chest, she grabbed up Sam's jeans and held them against her heart. Clung to his old clothes as if they were a replacement for the man.

"You're so stupid, Andrea Hamilton," she muttered. "Still pining away over a man you can't have, so stop thinking about him. *Stop it!*"

"Did you find what you're looking for?"

Still clutching the jeans in her arms, Andrea stiffened. With her back to the door, she could only hope Sam hadn't witnessed her foolishness, hadn't heard her declaration.

Glancing over her shoulder, she thankfully found his eyes focused on the open cedar chest, not her. He strolled over with hands in his pockets, then hovered above her like some dark, imposing monument to sheer male beauty.

He nodded toward the jersey laid out on top of the other items. "I remember Paul wearing that often."

Andi tossed the jeans aside and shifted to where she could get a better look at Sam, his reaction. He hid his emotions behind that steel facade, those impenetrable eyes. Tearing her gaze away, she leaned forward again and produced another keepsake. "Do you remember this?"

Sam crouched beside her and took the baseball from her grasp, turning it over and over with his strong fingers. His expression mellowed with remembrance. "I recall this very well. My first major league game. Cleveland Indians. In April, the year Paul and I met."

"And Paul caught the ball after a two-run homer."

Sam grinned. "The ball rolled from two rows above us and landed at his feet. It was a foul, not a home run. Paul thought the other story sounded more favorable."

Andi laughed. "That was just like him, making up something that sounded more exciting."

"Yes. Exactly like him." Sam's tone turned weary and so did his eyes.

When he tried to hand the ball back to her, she said, "Keep it."

"I could not—"

"He'd want you to have it, Sam. Besides, you two didn't bother to take me along, so why would I want it?"

His smile reappeared. "We did not take you because Paul worried that you would distract me from the game."

"He did not!"

"Perhaps he was not worried, but I was, the reason I didn't encourage your attendance."

Andi's face flushed hot as a summer sidewalk. "Always the charmer," she murmured.

"It's the truth, Andrea. You were very distracting. You still are."

Determined to move away from that topic, Andi patted the wooden floor next to her. "Have a seat. There's something else I need to give you."

Sam joined her on the floor, his long legs crossed the same as hers, and set the ball beside him. Andi reached into the corner of the chest and found the present in the same place she'd left it years before. The newspaper was yellowed, the blue bow tied around it somewhat flat. Tucked underneath the ribbon was an envelope that read "Sam, The Man."

She offered it to him. "It's Paul's graduation gift to you. I found it in his room when we were converting it to Chance's nursery."

Sam took it from her and placed the present in his lap. Andi noticed a slight tremor in his fingers when he slit open the envelope and withdrew the card. While he read to himself, his expression took on a pain so intense it stole Andi's breath.

"What does it say?" she asked.

He handed her the card and she, too, read in silence.

Hey, Sam. Just a little something for you to take back home. I'd send Andi with you, but she'd just give you grief. So I'm keeping her here for the time being, unless you decide to come back and take her off my hands. Seriously, if anything should happen to me, take care of her. She deserves to be happy.
Remember me.
Your bud, Paul

Tears burned Andi's eyes. Her throat ached and her

chest contracted with the sorrow that she'd kept at bay for more days than she could count.

"He knew," she said, her voice shaking with the effort to hold back the threatening tide of emotions.

"Knew what?"

She raised her eyes from the card to Sam. "When we were cleaning out his things, we also found two Christmas presents, one for me and one for Tess. Paul never shopped until Christmas Eve. I think he knew what was going to happen."

Sam sighed. "Andrea, I refuse to believe that Paul would drink himself to death, take his own life."

"That's not what I'm saying. Tess calls it 'angels' intuition.' The ability to know your fate."

"And you believe this?"

"I think anything's possible." Or she had at one time.

Andi glanced at the unopened package still resting in his lap. "Are you going to see what's inside?"

He carefully tore away the paper, revealing a framed photo that Tess had taken of Andi standing between Sam and Paul, arms wrapped around each other's waists, all three sporting bright grins on their dirt-spattered faces, the result of a mud-slinging contest after the boys had dumped Andi in the trough.

They all looked so happy, carefree. If only they'd known what the future held. If only they'd played a little longer, clung to each other a little tighter, told each other what they were feeling inside....

Andi could no longer hold back the tears. They fell at will, rolled down her cheeks and onto her T-shirt. Sam wrapped his strong arms around her, absorbing her sobs against his solid chest. He rocked her back and forth as she had rocked his son so many nights. She didn't want to need his consolation, his strength, but she did. She needed *him,* more than she should.

Tipping her face up, Andi brushed a kiss across his jaw, knowing that he could very well refuse this kind of comfort. But the possible benefit outweighed the probable rejection. Yet he didn't push her away. Instead, he cupped her face in his palms and kissed her. All the sadness melted away and desire took its place, as it had before.

Oh, how she remembered this, his gentle persuasion, the soft glide of his tongue, the velvet feel of his lips, his extraordinary skill. Those memories had served her well. No one had kissed her this way before or since. No one.

Sam abruptly broke the kiss, pushed away from her and stood. "I apologize," he said, sounding like the prince, not the man.

Andi felt angry, ashamed, weak. She lowered her eyes to the discarded photo and card, reminders that the kiss had come about from Sam's need to provide comfort and perhaps receive some comfort in return, not his need for her. From grief, not from desire. Although they were in a dusty attic, not stretched out by a pond, history seemed intent on repeating itself.

"This cannot happen again, Andrea," he stated, then quickly left the room without the jeans, Paul's gift or the baseball. Left Andi alone to mull over what to do about Samir Yaman.

She agreed it shouldn't happen again if she wanted to protect her heart, even if she still wanted him, and she did. Regardless, she had to accept that he was here, at least for the time being, and she needed to deal with it.

Andi gathered the jeans and laid the picture and card on top, then on second thought, grabbed the baseball in her free hand. She stood and sprinted down the stairs to find Sam standing in the second-floor hallway beside the attic entry, his forehead tipped against the wall.

"Here," she said, offering him the jeans. "Try these on. Maybe they still fit."

He pushed off the wall with both palms and faced her. "I doubt they will, at least at the moment."

When her confusion cleared, Andi lowered her eyes to the evidence below his belt stating loud and clear that he wasn't at all unaffected by the kiss.

She raised her gaze to his espresso eyes that expressed self-consciousness and, amazingly, the same desire she had seen the night he'd made love to her.

Maybe this was the answer. By making love with him again, maybe she could somehow, some way get him out of her system, find out for certain if the precious memories were nothing more than the imaginings of a girl who had turned to a man during her sorrow. Not love, only a need for solace.

She doubted Sam would be so quick to accommodate her, but that certainly didn't mean she couldn't try to persuade him, beginning now.

She shoved the jeans and photo against his chest, forcing him to take them from her. Then, with a courage she didn't know she possessed, she rolled the baseball slowly down his groin and slipped it into his pocket. Before she retreated, she ran a fingertip over the obvious bulge below his belt. "If you need any help with this, let me know."

With that she hurried to the first floor, not daring to look back to see his reaction. Before she made it out the door, she heard what sounded like a baseball hitting plaster, and she figured she'd probably driven home her point. Now she would attempt to drive him crazy with need, drive him back into her arms, and in doing so, drive him from her heart for good.

She'd have to take it slowly, plan carefully and, most important, remember she intended to tell him goodbye, once and for all.

Sam sat at the breakfast table, exhausted from physical labor and lack of sleep. After the way Andrea had touched him two days before, the kiss, the promise in her words, he had stayed awake both nights in Tess's room, tensing at every sound, worried that Andrea might come to him and he might not be able to turn her away. But in fact she had barely spoken to him as she carried on with her normal activities, not once mentioning the kiss or her proposition.

Sam had avoided her, but he couldn't avoid her now, especially when she occasionally glanced at him while moving the scrambled eggs around on her plate. He found himself staring at her mouth several times, watched while she nibbled at her food. Everything about her enthralled him, from the slight spattering of freckles across her nose, to the fragile column of her throat and that same fire in her eyes that caused his heart to pound in a fearsome rhythm.

He had tried to listen for the sound of the transport scheduled to bring the filly, but he hadn't been able to concentrate. Before, the family dog, an Australian shepherd named Troubles, would have alerted everyone. Odd, he hadn't noticed until today that the dog was no longer around.

Pushing his plate back, he asked, "Where is Troubles?"

Tess shook her head and spoke around a bite of toast. "He ended up on the wrong side of a tire when Chance was four."

"And you haven't found another?"

"I haven't had time," Andrea said as she stood.

Or the money, Sam thought. "I could provide one."

Andrea picked up their plates and slipped them in the sink. "That's not a good idea. With the traffic on the highway, I'm afraid we might lose another dog, and I don't want to put Chance through that again."

Sam hated the thought that his son had suffered through such a loss, but he was coming to realize that loss was a part of life that could not be avoided. "Then he remembers?"

Tess swiped at her mouth with a napkin. "Yeah, he remembers, but he's okay with it. Andi told him that Troubles was with Uncle Paul, jumping from star to star."

Obviously, Andrea still maintained a fascination with stars. The night Paul died she'd insisted that the brightest held his soul, and that she would hang her dreams on him for safekeeping. In that moment Sam had recognized that his love for her was as infinite as those stars. Making love with her had been a natural expression, a means to show her, since he had never told her.

The sound of a truck brought him out of his recollections and back into the present.

Andrea wiped her hands on a towel and faced him. "Do you think that's them?" Her excitement came through in her tone and the widening of her blue eyes. The first time Sam had witnessed her joy since Chance had left.

"Perhaps we should go see."

Before he could move, Andrea had already raced down the hall toward the front door.

"I swear," Tess said, then chuckled. "Nothing gets that girl more excited than a good horse."

Sam knew all too well what else excited her, but he would be wise to keep that out of his mind. "True. I hope this one doesn't disappoint her."

Tess propped her legs on the opposing chair and sent him a wicked grin. "I doubt she'll be disappointed. I'm sure you'll see to that while you're here, if you haven't already."

Without response Sam left the room, determined to ignore Tess's veiled suggestion. Nothing would please him more than to please Andrea in every way possible. But he would have to settle for providing a prize filly, otherwise he would be repeating past mistakes, knowing that he would have to leave her once again.

He joined Andrea at the rear of the massive trailer and waited for the filly to be unloaded. Sam was more than a bit apprehensive since he had never purchased a horse sight unseen. But when the man backed the filly down the ramp, Sam acknowledged that she was a treasure, as was Andrea who stood staring at the two-year-old. The woman had wonder in her eyes as she watched the filly prance about, restless with the need to run after her journey.

"Sam, she's unbelievable," Andrea said, almost in a whisper.

"I have to agree."

The man held the lead rope up. "She's all yours."

When Andrea failed to move, Sam said, "What are you waiting for?"

Andrea stepped forward and took the rope, then allowed the filly to sniff her free hand before scratching her behind the ears. As if the horse somehow knew she had found a friend, she settled down, accepting the display of affection without protest.

"What's her name?" Andrea asked.

"At the stables we called her Sunny," the man said. "Her registered name is Renner's Sun Goddess."

"Sunny it is." Andrea turned the horse and led her toward the stable. "I'm going to put her on a longe line and see how she moves," she tossed over one shoulder.

"Good," Sam said. "I'll join you in a moment."

By the time Sam had signed the appropriate paperwork and paid the handler before sending him on his way, Andrea had the filly in the outdoor arena, working her at a trot.

Sam propped one heel on the arena's bottom rung and watched both horse and trainer in action. The mare's flaxen mane and tail flowed with her fluid movements. Andrea's red-gold hair fluttered in the June breeze, the color very close to the horse's near-copper coat. Together they were a matched set, a tribute to beauty and grace with a wildness that lingered immediately below the surface.

Sam kept his attention on the filly only a brief moment, now that he had the opportunity to look his fill at Andrea without her knowledge. She had matured into a woman in every way, and that concept unearthed a searing heat low in Sam's belly that had nothing to do with the Kentucky sun.

She wore a light-blue shirt that barely reached the top of her jeans, jeans that fit every curve to perfection. When she raised her arm to keep the filly moving, Sam caught a glimpse of flesh at her waist. He imagined how it would feel to have his hands there, lower still, molding them to her bottom, pulling her against him, letting her know how strongly she could affect him, how being in her presence aroused him beyond all bounds. He was definitely aroused now and had been for two miserable days with no possible end to that misery, unless...

No, he could not act on those desires. It would be unfair to both of them, even though Andrea had made the offer of her assistance in that matter.

Andrea drew the filly into the center of the arena, turned to face him and called, "She's a winner, Sam."

Her vibrant smile had him smiling, too. Pleasing her did please him, and again he thought of many ways he could bring her more satisfaction, ways that would leave them clinging to each other, breathless, sated....

The crunch of gravel turned Sam's attention to the drive. A massive red truck pulled up next to the pen and a man dressed in typical cowboy garb got out.

Without invitation he opened the gate to the round pen and joined Andrea.

Because of his proximity, Sam couldn't hear the conversation though he assumed they were discussing the filly. Then their shared laughter floated over the breeze, and the man moved closer to Andrea. Too close.

Sam despised the sudden intimacy between them, hated even more that the cowboy touched Andrea's face then patted her bottom as if he had the right to do so. It took all of Sam's strength not to scale the fence and go after the idiot with fists raised. Luckily the man turned and left before Sam acted on that impulse. He had no cause to intervene. Andrea could do as she pleased with any man she pleased.

Still, Sam couldn't seem to get a grasp on his anger. It stayed with him all the way to the barn as he followed Andrea and the filly. The sway of her hips only fueled his fury when he thought about the man touching her with such intimacy, any man aside from him.

Once inside, Andrea turned the filly loose in the stall and came out holding a water bucket.

Sam leaned back against the opposite stall, hands fisted at his sides, no longer able to maintain his silence. "Who was that man?"

Andrea kept her back to him while she gathered the hose and began to fill the bucket. "Caleb? He's a friend."

"Only a friend?"

She regarded him over one shoulder. "The bay gelding at the end of the aisle is his. He stopped by to check on his progress. He's letting me have him for thirty more days for the basics, before he takes him to a cutting horse guy.''

"Then you're saying that his only interest in you has to do with your training skills?"

She shut off the water and turned, the hose still clutched in her fragile hand. "Of course."

"Are you still so naive, Andrea?"

Her face melded into a frown. "About what?"

"That man has designs on you as a woman."

She rolled her eyes. "Get off it, Sam. Caleb wants me to train his horse and that's all."

"He wants *you*, Andrea."

"Good grief. What on earth makes you think that?"

"The way he touched you."

"Touched me?"

"Are you saying you didn't notice when he put his hand on your…on your…butt?"

When Andrea laughed, Sam's temper flared again. "You find this funny?"

After recovering somewhat, she said, "I'm laughing because your assumptions about Caleb are ridiculous."

"My observations cannot be denied."

She tossed the hose to the ground. "You sound like a jealous lover."

Sam acknowledged that fact, but he couldn't stop his reaction. "Is *he* your lover, Andrea?"

Her eyes narrowed with anger. "That's really none of your business."

Regardless, Sam had to know. "Is he, Andrea?"

She leaned back against the stall. "Let me ask you

something. Have you been celibate all these years, Sam?''

"That's not the point.''

"Oh, I think it is. If we're going to get into my business, then that gives me the right to get into yours.''

"I'm concerned about our son," Sam said, grasping for anything so he would not have to admit there had been other women, but not so many as she might think, and none that could compare to what he had found with her. "I'm wary of those who would enter your life but have no intention of treating Chance appropriately.''

"If you must know, I've dated a couple of men, but it didn't work out because Chance didn't like either of them. For me that's the test. Chance's approval. Now are you satisfied?''

Only one thing would satisfy him, kissing the defiance from her expression, making her lips soften beneath his. "Obviously, this Caleb would like to be the next in line.''

"Your imagination is running wild, Sheikh Yaman.''

She was driving him wild, her eyes now as blue as flames. Sam wanted to touch her, to make her forget the fool who'd had his hands on her earlier. To forget every man she had ever let touch her. Yet he didn't dare give her more than advice.

"Your clothing leaves little to the imagination, Andrea. I suggest that you consider how you dress from now on.''

"I'm wearing what I wear every day of the week. Plain jeans and T-shirt.''

"Tight jeans and a very thin T-shirt."

She took a visual journey from his chest to the boots he had bought on a trip into town yesterday. "I'm thinking you've got the tight jeans market cornered. But I have to admit they look pretty darned good. I'm still surprised they fit."

They did, but barely, and the fit at the moment was less than comfortable. "My attire is not the issue at present." His gaze slid to her breasts. "You have on no bra. How can you expect a man to ignore this?"

She grabbed the hem of her shirt and pulled it out. "This provides plenty of cover."

"It shows far too much. Hides too little." Made Sam ache.

"I don't have that much to see, Sam. But thanks, anyway."

"You are wrong, Andrea. Wrong and foolish to think otherwise."

Her sudden smile caught him off guard. "Does this plain old T-shirt get your blood pumping, Sheikh Yaman?"

He couldn't deny that. "It is practically transparent."

She reached down and picked up the bucket. Sam believed she meant to carry it into the filly's stall. Instead she tipped it toward her, spilling the contents down the front of her, then tossed the bucket aside. She pointed at her breasts. "Now, this is transparent."

Sam could only stare at the dark shading of her nipples that showed through the saturated material. His hands opened and closed with the urge to touch her.

"Like what you see, Sam?" she asked, her tone full of challenge that he dared not answer.

But he couldn't keep from answering. He spanned the space between them before his brain registered that he had moved. Yet his body was very aware that he now had Andrea against the stall. He took her mouth without consideration of the consequences, thrusting his tongue between her parted lips with the force of his need while his hands searched beneath the wet fabric to cup both of her breasts. She whimpered when he thumbed each peak. Her hips ground against him in a torturous rhythm that made him hard and aching, balanced on the point of losing all restraint. He wanted to take her right there, right then, without regard to location or lack of privacy.

When she raised her arms, Sam pulled the drenched shirt over her head and dropped it to the ground behind her back while he trailed a path of wet kisses down the valley of her breasts. She arched her back, and her chest rose and fell rapidly in sync with his pounding heart, then her breath completely stopped when he drew one nipple into his mouth.

So lost in the taste of her dampened flesh, in the feel of her softness against his tongue, it took him a moment to notice the downward track of his zipper. Realization caught hold and he clasped her wrist.

"No, Andrea." He stepped back, away from her, then realized, with her standing there bare from the waist up, he was in danger of forgetting himself once again.

Yanking his own shirt over his head, he held it against her, shielding her from his eyes. "Put this on."

"But—"

"Put it on."

When she finally took the shirt, Sam walked to the opposite stall, braced his hands above his head and leaned into them. His chest burned from the effort it took to recover his breath and to calm his body.

When he turned again, thankfully she had honored his request. The knit shirt hit her at the knees, but the sharp sting of awareness was still present within him, even though she was now completely covered.

"I promised myself this would not happen between us," he said, his voice thick with the desire that he couldn't disregard.

She folded her arms across her breasts. "Wouldn't be the first time you've broken a promise, Sam."

"What promise have I broken?"

She strolled down the aisle a few steps then turned. "That night at the pond, you promised you wouldn't leave me."

"I meant that moment, Andrea. That night. Not forever."

"That's not at all how it seemed."

Sam recognized that he probably had led her to believe that he had meant always, bringing about more guilt. "I said many things to you that night, but we were both in pain." Lost in each other, lost in love both timeless and forbidden.

"Then you didn't mean any of it?"

He had meant most of it, but he hadn't stopped to consider that he couldn't keep those promises. "With you in my arms, I had forgotten who I was, what was expected of me. I regret that I was such a fool."

Andrea shrugged. "Guess that goes for both of us. Except there's one thing I don't regret."

"What is that?"

"Our son. Having him made Paul's death more bearable, easier to accept that you had left for good. I thank you for that gift. For him."

Sam doubted that he could feel any worse, any lower. "I regret that I have not been here for him, or for you."

"And you're going to have to leave us again. Do you regret that?"

More than she would ever know. "I do not have the luxury to dwell on regrets, Andrea. I've very little time left to know my son before I have to return home."

"Then why don't we make the best of that time together?" She sent him another lazy smile. "Do what comes naturally."

Sam clenched his jaw tight. "If you are saying that we should make love, then that would be unwise."

She moved closer to him, almost close enough for him to touch her again. It took all his fortitude not to reach out to her once more, finish what they had begun.

"In case you haven't noticed, Sheikh Yaman, I'm a grown woman now, not a girl. I'm not going to fall apart when you leave." Her gaze faltered, belying her confident tone. "So just in case you decide to change your mind…"

She brushed past him and headed toward the tack room. After a moment she came out and called, "Catch."

Sam grabbed the baseball midair, confused. "And the point to this is?"

She smiled a devious smile. "Just wanted to let you know that the offer still stands, in case you decide to play ball. Unless, of course, you can't handle it."

He could not handle hurting her again, and he would, once he told her the reasons why he could not stay.

She pivoted on her booted heels and swayed toward the barn's opening. Without turning around, she said, "Water the horse, will ya? I seem to be a little clumsy this morning."

For the second time in as many days, Sam slammed the ball against the wall, thinking it might be best if he did the same to his head. Perhaps he could pound Andrea out of his brain.

But a thousand blows and a million years would not begin to force Andrea Hamilton from his heart.

Four

When Andi stepped through the back door, she was suddenly assaulted by a cold draft of air and a strong case of chills. But it wasn't the air-conditioned kitchen that had her shivering, or her still-damp skin. Sam was the cause of her present condition.

She could still feel his soft abrading tongue on her breasts, his hands molding her bottom, his body pressed intimately against hers. Just thinking about him made her feel feverish, the low throbbing ache having yet to subside.

Andi hugged her arms across her chest, a sorry replacement for Sam, but she needed to hide the effects of their recent interlude. She realized all too late that she couldn't escape her aunt's scrutiny.

Standing at the sink, Tess grabbed a towel from the counter and surveyed Andi from chin to toes. "Correct me if I'm wrong, but wasn't Sam wearing that shirt this morning?''

Heat skimmed up Andi's throat and settled on her face. At the moment she felt like a schoolgirl caught necking in the pasture. Okay, so it wasn't the pasture, but it was pretty darned close. ''I had a mishap with the water bucket. He lent me his shirt since mine was soaked.''

Tess's knowing grin appeared. ''You two already having to cool yourselves off after just three days?''

She released a sigh. ''Don't let your imagination run away with you, Tess.'' Andi's, on the other hand, was long out of the starting gate and still running full-steam ahead, thanks to Sam.

Tess's forehead wrinkled from a frown as her gaze settled on Andi's mouth. ''I'm not imagining the whisker burn on your face, little girl. I might be old, but I'm not stupid.''

Andi walked to the cabinet and retrieved a glass. Her hands shook as she tried to fill it with water. ''I didn't say you're stupid, Tess. I'm just saying don't make too much out of this.''

''I won't if you won't. In fact, I think it's best if you stop and consider what you're doing before you make another mistake.''

Andi glanced up from the cup to Tess, who now looked considerably more serious. ''I don't consider Chance a mistake, Tess, if that's what you're suggesting.''

Tess leaned against the counter looking primed for a parental lecture. ''Of course he's not a mistake. He's been a godsend. But getting involved with Sam would be a mistake. He won't stay this time, either, Andi. You'd do well to remember that."

If only Tess realized that's all Andi had thought about the past few days. She didn't need to be reminded that Sam would leave once again in the name of duty to his country. Knowing didn't make it any easier to deal with, yet she was determined to keep everything in perspective. She also didn't expect Tess to understand what she intended to do—make love with Sam in order to get him out of her system.

"By the way," Tess said as she swiped at the kitchen counter, "the camp called."

Andi's chest tightened with panic, and she nearly dropped the glass. "What's wrong?"

"Nothing's wrong. They called to remind you about parents' day on Saturday. You have to be there by 8:30 a.m."

Relief flowed through Andi knowing that her baby was okay. After taking a long drink, she dumped the water into the sink and set the glass aside. "I remembered it was this weekend, but I didn't know I'd have to be there quite that early. I guess I can ask Sam to feed and water the horses."

Tess tossed the towel aside and faced Andi, her expression no less stern. "I'll feed the horses. Sam should go with you."

The panic returned to Andi once more. "I can't do that, Tess. Chance might start asking questions. He doesn't need to deal with any stress while he's away."

"And when do you intend to tell him, Andi? Never?"

She hadn't gotten that far in her thinking. She only

knew she didn't want to deliver any confessions during her son's first opportunity to establish his independence. ''I don't know when I'll tell him. Soon, I guess. Before Sam leaves.''

Tess sighed. ''That's up to you, but I still think Sam should go with you.''

''Where are you proposing I go?''

Andi tensed at the sound of Sam's deep voice coming from behind her. Trapped like a caged rabbit. She had no choice but to tell him about the event.

After facing Sam, Andi's well-rehearsed smile disappeared when she immediately contacted his bare chest, now at eye level. Her gaze skimmed over the territory marked by sinewy muscle and scattered with dark hair. Her fingers opened and closed with the urge to explore as if they'd been offered a masculine playground designed with a needy woman in mind.

In the barn she hadn't taken the time to study the details. In fact, she'd intentionally *avoided* the details after Sam thwarted her seduction. But she couldn't ignore them now, though she thought it best to stop looking with Tess playing audience.

She put on a casual smile and pulled her gaze back to his face. ''Actually, it's no big deal really. The camp is holding a parents' day on Saturday.''

His brows drew down into a frown. ''Parents' day?''

She shrugged. ''You know, games, a barbecue, that sort of thing. Pretty boring stuff.'' Especially for a man like Sam who probably spent his days in some elaborate palace surrounded by jewel-encrusted bowls of fruit and scantily clad women provided for his entertainment. She almost laughed over the absurdity of that stereotypical image, and silently cursed to think it might be an accurate assumption.

Forcing the thoughts away, she turned her attention back to Sam and noted her drenched shirt gripped tightly in his grasp. "I would like very much to go," he said.

"You would?"

"Yes. It would provide the opportunity to spend more time with my son."

"Exactly what I was thinking," Tess said.

Andi quelled the urge to tell her aunt that no one had asked her opinion on the matter. "I'm still not sure it's a good idea. Chance might wonder why you're there."

Sam's features turned tightrope tense. "You may tell him I'm there as a friend. I will not force you to say anything more, if that's your concern."

The anger and hurt in his tone made Andi flinch internally. She had already denied him many opportunities to know his child, though not intentionally. After all, *he* had been the one to disappear from their lives. He had been the one to discard her as if what had existed between them meant nothing at all.

Still, she had to consider Chance's opportunity to know his father. "I'll think about it." And she would, long and hard.

Tess brushed past Andi on her way toward the hall. "I'll leave you two alone to discuss it while I sit on the porch and snap some peas."

After Tess left the kitchen, Sam offered her the soggy T-shirt. "Perhaps you would like to return my clothes to me."

Andi couldn't suppress a devilish smile. "Do you want to do it now?"

"Do what?"

"Exchange shirts." She took a few steps and stopped immediately before him, close enough to touch the copper surface of his bare skin. "Unless you need something else from me?"

He released a frustrated sound, somewhere between a growl and a groan. "I prefer you stop making offers I cannot accept."

Determined to keep his attention, she ran a fingertip down his sternum along the stream of dark hair, and paused at his navel. "You can't accept them or you won't?"

"We've been through this, Andrea. I am not able to accept."

She sent a quick glance at the proof that he was still willing to play along. "You seem more than able to me."

He held her hand against his belly and kept his gaze fixed on hers as he exhaled slowly, his muscles tightening beneath her palm. Andi held her breath, wondering if this time he might decide to accept her offer. Maybe this time he would give up and give in, knowing this was what they both wanted. Even though he tried to deny that he did want her, she wasn't too dumb to read the signs. His eyes were dark, almost desperate, warring with indecision and desire. A slight sheen of perspiration covered his chest and forehead. His respiration sounded unsteady.

No, she wasn't too dumb to recognize that he wasn't at all unaffected, either here in the kitchen, or earlier in the barn. As affected as he had been seven years ago.

"Is this really all you want from me, Andrea?" he asked in a low, controlled voice as his fingertips stroked her knuckles. "This and nothing more? And afterward, will you then be satisfied?"

"Yes, I will," she said in a voice she didn't recognize.

He pushed her hand away and took a step back. "Perhaps you will, but I will not. If I have you, I promise I would want you more than once, and often, until I again must leave. Ask yourself truthfully if you would want to make love knowing nothing more will ever exist between us."

With that he tossed her wet shirt onto the table and strode out of the room, leaving Andi to ponder his words, the raw truth she heard in them. If she did have him once again—all of him—would it ever be enough?

There would never be enough time now.

Sam tossed his cell phone onto the sofa next to him and sent a string of mild curses directed at his duties. According to his father, the current situation in Barak demanded Sam return home immediately. Sam had bargained for two more weeks instead of four, on the pretense that he still had investments he needed to oversee. Only one week to spend with his son upon his return. Never enough time.

He shoved the newspaper's financial section off his lap, then scolded himself for acting like a child in the throes of a tantrum. Anger wouldn't serve him well at this time. He could only make the best of a situation beyond his control.

"Problems, Sam?"

Sam watched as Andrea strolled into the room and dropped down onto the sofa next to him, wearing a guarded expression and a pair of silk pajamas the color of fine champagne. The scent of orchids filtering into his nostrils served to make him forget his current troubles as did the sight of her dressed in feminine attire. Yet he refused to let her distract him. Now that he'd learned he would have to leave sooner, he had much to discuss with her.

"I'm afraid I must cut my visit short. I have been summoned home."

Her blue eyes widened. "Tonight?"

"No, but I will not be able to stay as long as I'd intended. I must return in two weeks."

Seeming to relax somewhat, she tucked her legs beneath her and sipped a glass of iced tea. "Was that Rashid on the phone calling to deliver the good news?"

"I spoke with my father. It is his wish that I return."

She frowned. "Do you always do what he tells you to do?"

Sam had expected her disapproval, but he hadn't expected her forthright query. "I have obligations, Andrea. Surely you understand, now that you have a child."

"I don't see Chance as an obligation," she said, ire in her tone. "I see him as a joy, not as a chore or a servant."

Sam lowered his eyes to his hands, clasped tightly

in his lap, biting back the sudden surge of anger. "Would you expect me to ignore my responsibilities?"

"I'd expect that being a prince might make you a little happier."

His gaze snapped to hers. "On what do you base this assumption, that I'm not happy with what I am?"

She shrugged. "You don't look happy, not like before. I've rarely seen you smile, much less laugh. In fact, most of the time you look way too serious. That's not the Sam I remember."

Sheikh Samir Yaman had replaced the Sam she remembered. The Sam she had known had yet to be tainted by the responsibility placed on his shoulders as the eldest son of a king. "That carefree college student you knew no longer exists."

"Oh, I think he's still in there just dying to get out."

"Unfortunately, that is not the case."

She set her glass on the coffee table before them and hugged her knees to her chest. "I'd hate to think that's true, Sam. I'd also hate to think that Chance would ever be subjected to the kind of pressure that would make him lose his spirit and his love of life."

If the truth were known, so would Sam. "I doubt that he will ever lose those attributes considering his mother."

Andrea's smile curled the corners of her beautiful mouth. "I suppose that's a compliment."

"Yes, very much so. I greatly appreciated your free spirit, your passion for living."

"And I appreciated your passion, too."

Sam was inclined to believe that she meant the passion they had experienced in each other's arms. He refused to travel that road of regret tonight, not with her so near, looking like temptation incarnate. He wasn't that strong.

He cleared his throat and leaned back against the sofa, hoping to seem relaxed when in fact he was anything but. "I have learned to deal with the demands of my station. It is who I am."

"It's a title, Sam, not who you are. My father never tried to make me something I'm not. Neither did Paul. They just let me be myself."

"If my memory serves me, Paul once said that it would take a front-end hauler, a steel cable and an ancient oak to tie you down."

Andrea tossed back her head and laughed, filling Sam with joy over the sound. "That's a front-end loader, and yes, he did say that, and I've heard you say worse. You guys were always teasing me. You lived to drive me nuts."

"You were an easy target."

She smiled. "A moving target most of the time, you mean. Especially when you both came at me and threatened to tickle me senseless."

Sam grinned at the memories. "I believe you have very sensitive knees."

Andrea hugged her legs tighter against her chest. "Don't you even think about it, mister."

He inched a little closer despite the voice that told him to keep his distance. "It might be amusing to see if that continues to hold true."

"Still the bully, just like before."

"Before it was the only way to make you do my bidding."

Her smile faded and her expression softened, taking on the appearance of a woman more than willing to submit to his demands. "That wasn't the only way."

Sam was suddenly catapulted back to that night at the pond. Never had any woman given him as much with such sweet abandon. And considering she'd been barely more than a child all those years ago, he could only wonder what she would be like now as a woman.

Inching closer until she was flush against his side, she brushed his hair away from his forehead. "Do you ever think about that night, Sam? Not about Paul, but about what happened between us?"

Even after seven years, those memories still haunted his dreams in sleep and his thoughts upon waking. "I remember."

"Do you ever wish that it hadn't happened?"

How could he explain so she would understand? He caught her hand and brushed a kiss across her palm. "I suppose that if I could change anything about that time, it would only be two things."

With fine fingertips she traced a path along his jaw. "What would they be?"

"That I could have saved Paul from his fate. And that I could have stayed."

Her face lit up as if he had offered her the stars that held her dreams. Leaning forward, she whisked a kiss across his cheek. "Thank you."

He did not deserve her gratitude, then or now. "Nothing has changed, Andrea. We cannot go back. I will still leave you again."

She framed his jaw in her slender fingers. "We could make up for lost time. There are a lot of hours in fourteen days."

Not nearly enough, Sam decided. Not nearly enough distance between them, either. Normally he was a man with a firm resolve, but Andrea unearthed his weakness, could mold him as easily as if he were made of clay. As he stared at her lips, he became caught in the grip of longing.

Sam claimed her mouth for a kiss fueled by a power he didn't know he possessed. In the far reaches of his mind, he realized he should be experiencing some guilt, since he was promised to another. But that woman was as unfamiliar to him as the concept of turning his back on his country and his legacy. He could only consider the sweet heat of Andrea's mouth, the gentle foray of her tongue against his, the feel of her lithe body curled against him as he deepened the kiss and tightened his hold on her.

The passion that was so much a part of Andrea came out in the kiss. Her hands roved over his back in steady strokes as if she were memorizing this moment. He caught a handful of her hair as if to moor himself against the onslaught of heat, of desperate desire. When she draped one leg over his thigh, he curved his palm over her waist. They parted for a moment, but only a moment, to draw air before their mouths united again. How easy it would be to touch her, Sam thought. How easy to show her pleasure. He slipped his hand between her thighs and Andrea wriggled her encouragement.

Reality soon caught hold and Sam became aware that if he continued, he would not be able to stop. He would toss away all his reasons for avoiding this very thing and carry her to bed, make love to her all through the night, destroying his determination not to hurt her more than he already had.

Breaking the kiss, he tipped his forehead against hers as he tried to regain his respiration. "You are still too hard to resist."

"Then why even bother?"

He pulled back and searched her blue eyes. "You know the reasons why. Because I—"

"Have to go back to the magic kingdom," she said, then scooted away from him to the other end of the sofa. "You don't have to remind me again."

"I'm glad you are finally beginning to understand."

She picked up a throw pillow and held it against her breasts. "Now that we've established you'll be leaving, for about the hundredth time, I've come to a decision."

"About?"

"Chance. I've decided you can go with me to the camp."

Sincerely pleased, Sam smiled. "Good. We can travel in the limo instead of that wreck you call a truck."

He snared the pillow she tossed at him in one hand before it hit his face. "What's wrong with my truck?"

"Nothing if you're hauling feed and hay and traveling only a short distance. I believe my mode of transportation provides more comfort and reliability. And if you'll recall, our son expressed his desire to ride in it. Rashid can drive us."

Andrea chewed her bottom lip for a moment before raising her eyes to his. "Maybe that is a good idea.

Plenty of room in the limo. Lots of room, in fact.'' She smiled once again. A smile that could only mean trouble for Sam. ''In fact, I just bet you could stretch out if you wanted to.''

''Andrea,'' he said in a half-warning tone, a great effort considering the arrival of visions of Andrea beneath him, naked, in the dimly lit limousine.

She stretched her arms above her head, giving him a good view of her breasts unencumbered beneath the satin, then rose and stood above him. ''Relax, Sam. I promise I won't make you do anything you don't want to do.''

Exactly what he feared, for if given the opportunity, Sam knew precisely what he would want to do—make love to her as if tomorrow would not arrive.

In many ways, at least in regard to his time with the mother of his child, that was very close to the truth.

''Got a minute to gab, Andi?'' Tess asked the following day.

Andi looked up from gathering a few things for the trip to camp and gave her attention to Tess. ''Sure. What's up?''

Pacing the length of the bedroom, Tess paused to toy with various keepsakes on the bureau. ''I have something I need to tell you.''

Andi tossed the picnic blanket aside and took a roost on the edge of the bed, gearing up for a ''Sam'' lecture. ''I've agreed to let him go with me, if that's what's bugging you.''

Tess finally faced her. ''I know. Sam told me. But this doesn't have a thing to do with him.''

Realizing Tess meant serious business, Andi patted the mattress beside her. "Have a seat and tell me what's got you in such a mood."

Tess joined her and wrapped an arm around Andi's shoulder. "Honey, Riley has asked me to marry him."

"So what else is new?"

"This time I said yes."

Andi's heart took a nosedive over the prospect of losing the one person she had come to count on through thick and thin, a proverbial port in the storm, her touchstone.

Hiding her selfishness with a smile, Andi proclaimed with a goodnatured pat on Tess's thigh, "Well it's about damned time."

Tess gave Andi's shoulder a motherly squeeze. "Then you're okay with this?"

"Are you asking my approval?"

"I'm asking how you feel about it."

Rising from the bed, Andrea took her place at the bureau where Tess had been a few moments before, her back turned to her aunt so she wouldn't give herself away. "Of course I'm okay with it. I'm thrilled." She didn't sound at all thrilled.

Biting back the tears, Andi drew in several cleansing breaths. Tess's careworn hands coming to rest on her shoulders almost proved to be her undoing.

"I know the timing seems pretty bad with Sam here again," Tess said, "but Riley bought himself one of those new-fangled homes on wheels and he wants to travel."

That brought Andi around to face Tess. "You mean you'll be gone all the time?"

"A lot of the time. We'd like to see the country in our golden years, before we're too old to enjoy it."

Andi attempted another smile, but her lips felt as stiff as a metal pipe. "That sounds great, Tess."

Tess tried to smile, as well, but it, too, seemed forced. "During the summers you and Chance can come along with us, when he's out of school."

"Oh, yeah, Tess. I'm sure Riley would love having us along while you're still on your honeymoon."

"Next year, silly girl. We're not going to tie the noose until after Sam leaves."

Andi shrugged. "Why not now? Sam can be Riley's best man. Heck, how many people can say they have a prince standing up for them during the nuptials?" Her attempt at humor rang false, and she realized her aunt saw right through her.

Tess brushed Andi's hair away from her shoulders, a gesture so endearing and familiar it made Andi's heart ache, and the stubborn tears threatened to appear once again. "Your time will come, Andi girl. You only have to open yourself up. You can do that once Sam's gone again."

Did everyone have to keep reminding her about Sam's impending departure? Was everyone so bent on believing that her world revolved around him?

Andi swallowed past the boulder in her throat, determined not to cry over something she couldn't control. "Whether Sam's here or not makes no difference to me, except where Chance is concerned. There's nothing more between us." If only Andi had sounded more convincing. If only she really believed that.

"There will always be something between you two, Andi. A child, and two different worlds. He can't give you what you need, but someday you'll find a man who can.''

Andrea wanted to stomp her foot and cuss like a ranch hand. She wanted to scream that this supposed ''special'' man didn't exist in any world, especially hers. Instead, she said, ''I'm satisfied with my life, Tess. My work and Chance are all I need. And I'm thrilled for you and Riley. You've been the only mother I've ever known, and if you hadn't been there when Daddy and Paul died, I don't know what I would've done. You deserve some happiness, too.''

Tess tugged her into a solid embrace. ''I'll always be here for you, honey, God willing.'' She pulled back and studied Andi's face through the eyes of a mother concerned for her child. ''Just like I was for all the hurts and heartaches, and for Chance's entry into this crazy world, I'll be there when your prince leaves again.''

Your prince. Andi had never been one to put much stock in fairy tales, or to believe that some knight would come along and rescue her. Sheikh Samir Yaman had shattered those dreams long ago, and he would shred her life again if she let him.

But she wouldn't let him destroy her. As always, she would survive. She and Chance together. Andi didn't need a prince, even one she would probably love forever.

Five

Sam regarded Andrea over the magazine he'd pretended to read for the better part of the trip to the camp. Thankfully she had retired early the night before without further mention of lovemaking. In fact, she had said very little at all, then and now. At the moment she sat across from him wringing her hands and staring with an unfocused gaze out the tinted window.

Curious over her uncharacteristic silence, Sam tossed the magazine aside and studied her. "Are you afraid that our son has forgotten his mother?"

She turned startled eyes on him. "Of course not. Why would you think that?"

"You seem very nervous."

She tightened the rubber band around her hair. "Can you blame me? I mean, I'm about to take you to camp. Even if Chance doesn't question your resemblance to him, other people are going to automatically assume you're his father.''

"That is not necessarily so.''

"Oh, come on, Sam. He looks just like you, right down to the blasted dimple.''

Sam couldn't contain his pride or his smile. "He has your nose.''

Andi placed her fingertips on the tip of her nose as if to verify that fact. "He does at the moment, but he's still just a baby. I'm sure he'll have your aristocratic honker by the time he's a teenager.''

"Honker?''

"That's what Chance calls noses.''

"You do not care for my nose?''

"Your nose is fine. Very sophisticated.''

"I am relieved it meets with your approval.''

Her grin came out of hiding. "Everything about you meets with my approval. All those parts seen and unseen, or as best I can remember, because it's been a while since I've seen all your parts.''

Sam shifted in his seat and resisted the urge to offer an inspection. At least they had survived the duration of this trip without utilizing the privacy of the limo. But on the ride home...

"Looks like we're here.'' The limo had barely come to a stop before Andrea slid out the door. Sam hurried out behind her, afraid she would abandon him and leave him to his own devices. He knew nothing about how he should act at this camp. He had no idea how to answer any questions that might arise about his relationship with Andrea and Chance. He would simply have to allow Andrea to handle the situation in the way she saw fit. He suspected he would not care for her explanations.

Sam caught up with Andrea immediately outside a large cedar cabin surrounded by several adults. A young woman approached them and held out her hand. "Hi, I'm Trish, Ms. Hamilton."

"Nice to meet you, Trish," Andrea replied politely.

"You don't remember me? We met when you came to check out the camp."

Andrea continued her hand kneading. "I'm sorry. It's been a long drive."

Trish seemed unfazed by Andrea's lack of memory and continued on at a vibrant pace. "We're glad you could come today. Chance is so excited. He's a fantastic little boy. Quite the happy camper."

Andrea's gaze roamed the immediate area. "Where is he?"

"In the dining hall finishing up breakfast. He'll be right out." Trish turned her smile on Sam. "And you must be Mr. Hamilton."

"His name is Mr. Yaman," Andrea added quickly. "A family friend."

The woman looked flustered. "Well, I'm sorry. It's just that Chance looks so much like you."

Andrea produced a nervous smile. "I know. Isn't that weird?"

Sam hated the denial, hated that Andrea didn't see a need for the truth. "Chance's father and I are from the same country," Sam offered along with his hand.

"Cool," Trish said after a brief handshake.

A spattering of laughter and shouts broke the awkward moment as myriad children came rushing out the doors of the largest cabin to the left.

"Mama! You came!"

Chance rushed Andrea and engaged her in a voracious hug. She picked him up and held him tightly against her breasts. "I've missed you, sweetie. Are you having fun?"

He squirmed in her grasp. "Yeah. Lots of fun. Put me down, Mom, before the other guys see."

Looking heartsick, Andrea complied but kept her hand on his shoulder. "Guess that wouldn't be cool," she said in a voice that sounded much like the camp counselor.

Chance stared up at Sam with surprise as if he'd only now realized his presence. "How come you didn't tell me you were bringing the prince?"

Andrea sent a quick glance at Sam, then said, "We only decided a few days ago."

Sam held out his hand. "I hope that is all right with you, Chance."

Chance displayed his approval with a jerk of his head and a hearty handshake. "Sure. Did you bring the car?"

Sam hooked a thumb over his shoulder. "In the parking lot."

His son's eyes grew large with wonder, reminding Sam of Andrea. "Can I take the guys for a ride?"

"Not now, sweetie," Andrea said. "Maybe before we head back. Right now we have to play some games."

Andrea took Chance by the hand and headed off toward the group of parents gathered at the flagpole. Sam stood in place watching mother and child walk away, hand in hand, without concern that they had left him behind. He despised feeling the outsider, welcome only because of his car—a symbol of his wealth—not as a part of this family.

Perhaps it would be best if Chance never knew the

truth. Perhaps he should walk away and never look back, knowing it would be favorable for everyone concerned, especially his son. Yet it would prove to be a most difficult choice.

Then suddenly Chance tugged his hand from Andrea's grasp and came running back to Sam. He toed the dirt beneath his feet then stared at Sam with eyes much like his own. "Can I ask you somethin'?"

Sam ruffled the boy's dark head. "Certainly."

"It's kind of a favor."

Kneeling on Chance's level, Sam's expression softened as did something deep inside him. "Do not be afraid to ask anything of me."

"Can you pretend to be my dad today?"

Andi hadn't minded that Chance requested Sam be his "pretend" father, even though it wasn't at all pretend. She hadn't minded that Sam seemed to garner all the attention during the day-long activities. After all, he was a prince. She hadn't minded that he had been chosen to anchor the tug-of-war rope for Chance's team since he was well built for the challenge. Nor had she really cared that Chance took great pains in introducing Sam to everyone while she seemed almost inconsequential. Besides, when Chance scraped his knee during the softball game, he had sought out his mother to kiss away the hurt.

Yet she couldn't help but feel a little jealous when Chance told Sam that he'd had the best time ever, even more fun than when Andi had entered him and his pony in the local Fourth of July parade. How could she compete with that?

She couldn't, and she shouldn't want to. In fact, she should be thrilled that father and son had hit it off. But she couldn't be totally happy, knowing that in a matter of days Sam would be gone from their lives, maybe even for good, before Chance really got to know him as his father.

While Rashid took one last circle around the parking lot in the limo accompanied by Sam, Chance and a half dozen other boys, Andi stood alone and waited patiently. She would give them these special moments together without complaint, knowing they might be some of the last.

The car came to a stop nearby and a group of chatty boys piled out, then headed off at a run toward the dining hall for the evening meal. Chance hung back to talk with Sam while Andi leaned into the limo to load her bag and blanket into the car. After she was done, she found Sam crouched on Chance's level near the trunk, explaining the finer points of Thoroughbred racing. Funny, Chance had never seemed to care all that much about Andi's explanations of the sport.

She approached quietly and rested her hand on Chance's hair still damp from their afternoon swim. "It's time for you to go on back, honey. Dinner's ready and we need to get home to check on the horses."

Chance looked up, disappointment in his eyes. "Okay. But can Sam pick me up in the limo next weekend?"

"I don't know, sweetie. You'll have to ask—"

"I will make it a point to be here," Sam interjected.

Andi pulled Chance into an embrace, thankful that he allowed it. "You be good."

"I will, Mom."

"Eat right and check your levels."

"Yeah, Mom."

"Be sure to get plenty of rest and—"

"Can I go now, Mother? I'm hungry."

Mother? Since when had she stopped being Mama?

After popping a kiss on his cheek, Andi released Chance knowing that she would eventually have to learn to let him go, something that was all too familiar where the men in her life were concerned.

Chance turned to Sam and gave him a high-five. "Later, Mr. Sheikh."

Sam grinned. "Later."

With a last wave, Chance set off toward the cabin, taking a tiny piece of Andi's heart with him.

Sam gestured toward the open door. "Shall we?"

Andi took another glance toward the cabin only to discover that her son had disappeared. "I guess so," she said, then slid inside the limo.

For the first few minutes they rode in silence, yet Sam couldn't seem to stop smiling. Andi reluctantly admitted she appreciated his joy and understood it. Spending time with your child was the greatest experience on earth.

"So did you have fun, Sheikh Yaman?" she asked in a teasing tone.

His grin deepened. "Yes, I did most certainly."

"I'm glad." Andi paused for a moment, frustrated that he was going to make her drag a conversation out of him. "I noticed you really seemed to enjoy the swim."

"Very much."

"The women sure seemed to enjoy watching you swim."

He frowned. "I do not understand."

"Are you saying you didn't notice they were all

staring at you when you rose from the water like some Arabian god?''

Sam laughed. ''Andrea, your imagination is second only to your love of good horseflesh.''

''I'm not imagining things. I thought I might have to do CPR on them when you executed that perfect dive. Of course, those swim trunks did tend to enhance your finer features.''

''They are plain, Andrea. Simple black. Adequate cover.''

''Nancy sure seemed to like them, and everything in them.''

He raised one dark brow. ''Nancy?''

''Yeah. Little Bubba's mother. The divorced one who wore four-inch heels with her metallic gold thong and kept gushing over you all day.''

''I do not remember her.''

''Oh, I'm so sure.''

His gaze slid over Andi, and she suddenly found herself covered in gooseflesh. ''I would not have noticed this Nancy with you present. The suit you wore drew attention, as well, and not from me alone. The blue brought out the color of your eyes and the fit enhanced your figure. Very nice indeed.''

Andi wanted to laugh. Her suit was a relatively modest two-piece, and for most of the day she'd worn her oversize cover-up. ''I just bet you say that to all the girls in your harem.''

''I have no harem.''

Andi tossed up her hands in mock exasperation. ''Well, darn. There went my desert fantasy.''

Sam rubbed a large hand down his thigh, bare because of the shorts he now wore, capturing Andi's attention. ''I am sorry to disappoint you.''

In reality he hadn't disappointed her. Yet. But the night was young, and she had only one major goal in mind—to convince Sam that spending the next two hours in the limo could be as boring, or as exciting, as they chose to make it.

On that thought, she fanned her face. "It's rather warm in here, don't you think?"

His expression went as taut as the black leather covering the seats. "I am comfortable."

"Well, I'm not." She unbuttoned her blouse and let it fall open to reveal the top of her less-than-comfortable bra. "That's a little better."

"I will ask Rashid to adjust the air." Depressing the intercom button to his right, he made the request then settled back against the seat with the magazine he'd been reading earlier.

This would not do, Andi thought. She refused to let him ignore her. Feeling brave, she reached for the button on her denim shorts then reconsidered. "Speaking of Rashid, can he see back here?"

Sam sent her a suspicious look. "Not as long as the privacy window is intact. Why do you ask?"

"Just wondering."

Muttering something in Arabic that Andi couldn't understand, Sam went back to the magazine and Andi went back to tugging off her shorts. On afterthought, she unfastened her bra and slipped it off through the armholes then tossed it onto the floor to join her shorts. Now she wore only a white sleeveless cotton shirt and a pair of skimpy black panties. If that didn't get his attention, Andi doubted anything would, short of leaning out the window naked and hollering at the top of her lungs.

When Sam failed to look at her, she decided to take

matters into her own hands, or whatever else she needed to take into her hands to earn his notice. All day long she'd endured the sidelong glances aimed at Sam. And all the while she'd had to pretend they were old friends.

She was tired of the whole charade because he was more than a friend. He was the father of her child, and at one time her lover. Just once more before he disappeared again, she wanted to experience all that he had to offer, if she could just convince him to cooperate.

On that thought, Andi slipped to her knees and crawled to the opposite seat to move between Sam's parted legs. When he looked up, she noted a hint of surprise in his expression.

She grabbed the magazine and tossed it behind her, then slipped her fingertips immediately underneath the hem of his khaki shorts. "Is that magazine so darned interesting that you can't give me a little of your time?"

He nailed her with his dark eyes. "Is my time all you want, Andrea? If so, you do not have to resort to such measures as crawling on your knees."

"You don't like me on my knees?" she asked, topped off with a suggestive grin.

His glance fell to her open blouse that now revealed a good deal of her breasts. "I would like you to return to your seat and put your clothes back on before I…"

His words trailed off, leading Andi to believe that he was entertaining some of the same naughty ideas.

"Before you what?"

"Before Rashid sees you."

She frowned. "I thought you said he couldn't see back here with the window up."

"I do not believe he can, but I've never ridden in the front to test the window's merits. It would be unwise to take that risk."

Andi's wicked side surfaced, and she climbed onto the seat on her knees, straddling Sam's thighs. "Why don't we just hope for the best? Besides, you can always say you had something in your eye and I was trying to remove it."

He braced his hands on her waist but didn't attempt to move her out of the way. "I doubt that Rashid would buy such a weak excuse."

"Considering this car's owner, I'd just bet Rashid has probably seen it all."

"What are you saying?"

"You and other women engaging in some hanky-panky."

"I use this car for business purposes and nothing more."

She rimmed her tongue along the shell of his ear and whispered, "Then maybe we should get down to business."

"Andrea, why are you so intent on pursuing this?"

Pulling back, she locked into his dark gaze, determined to have her say—and her way. "Because I have to know if I only imagined how wonderful you made me feel, or if it's just the fact I had no one to compare you to." She ran the tip of her tongue across the seam of his lips. "I want to know if you're really all that great."

Sam tightened his grip on her waist, and his eyes went almost black. "Are you saying that you wish to know how I compare to other men? Have there been so many, Andrea?''

There had been only one other man, a brief affair that had been more than disappointing, but revealing that fact wouldn't help her cause. ''I'm saying it was a long time ago and that maybe my recollections are incorrect.''

''Yet you have told me repeatedly you do not wish to resurrect the past.''

''I'm telling you now that I *need* you to refresh my memory.'' She moved against him, immediately noting the slight swell beneath her bottom. ''Is that a camel in your pocket, or are you just glad to see me?''

Sam's grin surfaced. ''You can be a very devious woman, Andrea.''

''You don't know the half of it, but I'd be glad to show you.''

Indecision warred in his expression. Andi knew the moment he lost the battle when he released a strained breath. ''Perhaps I should show you a few things.''

Sliding his hands to her hips, he pressed down until she could feel every glorious part of him. He nudged her forward then back ever so slightly against his erection, creating an amazingly erotic friction and a rush of damp heat where Andi's body contacted his.

''I remember much about that night,'' he said in a voice only a degree above a whisper, deep and grainy and sensual. ''I remember the way you looked, trusting and innocent. I remember how your skin felt beneath my hands.''

He slipped his hands beneath her panties and stroked her bare bottom. ''Do you remember me touching you this way, Andrea?'' He asked the question while continuing to glide her hips back and forth against him in a steady rhythm.

She combed her hands through his dark hair then closed her eyes. "Maybe."

Like some love-starved woman, she savored the feel of his mouth as he feathered a kiss across the rise of her breast, grazing his tongue over her nipple just enough to tease and entice. "I remember the soft sounds of pleasure you made when I kissed you this way, how you begged me to continue."

Right now she was primed for some more begging if he dared to stop. "It's beginning to come back to me, but I could use a little more detail." In reality, she hadn't forgotten one incredible detail.

He began to move his hips in sync with hers, increasing the contact of their bodies that fitted so perfectly together. "I remember how brave you were, how you ignored the pain."

The pain had been nothing compared to the pleasure. And the pleasure was upon her now as Sam continued his erotic motion, rubbing cotton against silk, creating delicious sensation against the place that needed his attention the most. He undid two more buttons on her blouse and a cool draft of air streamed over her bare breasts.

Andi kept her eyes closed, lulled by the sound of his sensual voice. "I remember how you trembled beneath me. How warm and wet and soft your body was surrounding mine. I remember being totally lost to you at that moment."

She remembered being lost, too. She was quickly losing her way once more, especially when he took her breast completely into his mouth and laved his tongue back and forth over her needy flesh. But it only lasted for a short time until he commanded, "Look at me, Andrea."

She opened her eyes slowly to find him staring at her intently as he began to speak again. "Do you remember how it felt to be so close?"

He tilted his pelvis upward, causing her to gasp. "Yes, I remember," she said with all the adamancy she could muster at such a moment.

"Do you remember what I told you?"

She could hardly breathe, much less think. "Tell me again, just in case I don't."

"I told you that I had never been so lacking in control. That I had never had such feelings or that I had never wanted a woman so badly."

Coherent words escaped her, but Sam's enticements came through loud and clear and compelling, his movements more insistent, bringing Andi to the brink, though he had yet to use his hands on her. And, oh, did she want him to do that very thing. But he continued his assault on her senses, touching her only with his words and heady movements. "I also recall that as I brought you to a release, you called my name."

And that's exactly what Andi did again as a searing climax overtook her. She literally saw stars this time, too, only they weren't those found in the night sky above them.

Andi collapsed against Sam's broad chest and shuddered uncontrollably while he held her close to his heart, which pounded a steady rhythm against her cheek. When the world finally came back into focus, she felt a little foolish. She also realized he had his palm over her mouth.

"No doubt Rashid heard that," he said, followed by a chuckle. "Do you feel inclined to shout again?"

She managed to shake her head no, still mute even after he dropped his hand from her mouth.

"Have I adequately jarred your memories?" he asked.

He'd done much more than that. "Every last one."

"Good." As if the interlude was an everyday occurrence, he set her aside and claimed the opposing seat.

Andi could only stare at him with mouth and shirt gaping until the shock subsided. "That's it?"

He had the nerve to look surprised. "That was not enough?"

She refused to let him off the hook until she had exactly what she'd been seeking since that first day he'd reentered her life. "I want you to finish this, dammit."

"It is finished, Andrea."

"You mean to tell me that you're willing to leave it at that? Even when you didn't—"

"That should not matter to you."

She sent a pointed glance at the obvious ridge beneath his shorts, proof positive that he still had issues he needed to settle. "It does matter to me. I want it all, and I'd bet all the hay in the barn that you want more, too."

"You want more than I can give you."

"I want sex, Sam. Hard, lusty limo sex. That's not too much to ask."

His eyes took on a solemn cast. "I want to leave knowing that I have done nothing to hurt you."

This time Andi wanted to scream with frustration instead of passion. "If you're worried about getting me pregnant, I've prepared for that.'' She yanked her bag from the floor and opened the zippered pocket to show him the condoms she had purchased the day before.

He still seemed totally immovable as he eyed the foil packets. ''That is a wise choice, Andrea, but have you considered how you will protect your heart?''

Anger impaled Andi soul deep, baring the wound that had festered like an inflamed blister for seven years. He still viewed her as that same girl who had hung on his every word, his every touch, too naive to know her own mind. That girl was long gone.

She gripped her open blouse with one hand and tossed the condoms back in the bag with the other. ''You just don't get it, Sam. I don't want anything except a quick roll. That's it. No promises of tomorrow. No *I love you*s. Heck, you don't even have to sleep in the same bed with me.''

The lie sat like a rock in her belly, but she was too proud to admit that she did want more. She wanted everything, not just sex. She wanted to be with him the next day and the next. She wanted him to be a part of Chance's life. But most of all she wanted his love, something she knew she would never have.

Six

He had sworn never to hurt Andrea again, yet that's exactly what he had done by acting as though touching her had meant nothing. In reality it had meant everything.

On the return home the silence in the car had been stifling, and as soon as they pulled up in the drive, Andrea had gathered her belongings and exited the car without speaking. Only, she had not returned to the house. But Sam knew precisely where she had gone.

He could not let so much go unsaid between them. He would need to attempt once more to explain why he could promise her nothing. Perhaps he should tell her about his impending marriage to Maila so she would understand his resistance. Though the young woman meant nothing to him, he felt honor bound to

his commitment. He doubted Andrea would understand, yet she needed to hear the truth.

As he set out on the path that led through the fields,
the air was heavy with mist, almost stifling, and so
were his thoughts as he silently rehearsed what he
would say to Andrea. But when he came upon her
seated on the blanket facing the pond, her elbows resting on bent knees and her beautiful face cast in the
light of a half-moon, everything he had thought to
say vanished.

Quietly he came up behind her and dropped to his
knees, then circled his arms around her. "I knew I
would find you here."

When she shuddered, he wondered if he should let
her go. Instead he held her tighter. "Are you cold?"
he asked.

"No. I'm just having a strong sense of déjà vu."

Sam moved around to face her and took her hands
into his. He was uncertain where to begin but decided
seven years ago would be an appropriate place to
start. "I am sorry for leaving you without an explanation after Paul's funeral. I feared that if you'd asked
me to stay, I wouldn't have been strong enough to
deny you, and I knew that I must."

She turned her face to the stars. "Let's not go there
tonight, Sam. You did what you thought you had to
do."

He drew in a sharp breath. "I do also wish to apologize for my behavior in the car. It was unfair to
you."

Inclining her head, she surveyed him a moment
with soulful blue eyes. "You've told me all along that

you don't want me, so you have nothing to be sorry for.''

He released a frustrated sigh. ''I do want you. I have never stopped wanting you.''

Her expression brightened somewhat, yet she still looked wounded. ''You have a strange way of showing it.''

He attempted a smile. ''I thought it was quite evident.''

Finally Andrea's smile returned, a smile that had stayed with him over many days. Would stay with him always. ''Okay, so maybe it was a little obvious.'' Her features went solemn once again. ''But that's just a physical reaction, Sam. It doesn't really mean anything.''

Framing her face in his palms, he said, ''You have no idea how much you mean to me. How much you have always meant to me. But I cannot promise you anything.''

''I told you I don't expect any promises.'' She pulled his hand away and held it against her breast. ''Life is so very short. No one can predict what will happen tomorrow. We both know that. I'm only asking for here and now. I just want to be with you. And when it's over, then we'll both move on with our lives knowing that we've found some joy in each other one more time.''

Sam considered what she was saying and then considered his marriage contract. Arrangement, he corrected. Only verbal to this point. His father had called because of that impending contract. Maila's father was growing impatient with his absence, a greedy man willing to sell his daughter into a union for the sake of finances.

Maila was several years younger and a virtual stranger to Sam. The two times they had met, she had barely spoken to him and only then to give her vow that she would try to produce a son although he sensed that prospect wasn't all that appealing to her. But Sam already had a son—a cherished child mothered by a woman for whom he cared deeply. A woman who now offered herself to him without condition. At the moment all he could consider was forgetting his obligations and turning his attention to that woman one last time.

"Are you certain you want this, Andrea?"

"Are you saying you're willing to consider it?"

"As I told you before, I fear hurting you."

"You'll only hurt me if you keep acting as if there's nothing going on between us, if you deny me this opportunity to be with you again in every way."

"Are you not worried that I will disappoint you?"

Rising from the blanket, she began once more to undo her blouse and slipped it completely away. She then removed her shorts and panties, leaving her cloaked only by the night. "Do I look worried to you?"

"No. You look exquisite." And she did, more captivating than he remembered. Priceless perfection. All his, if he so chose.

Heat surged through him and settled in his groin. A deep, abiding heat that made him hard and desperate to be inside her once more. That frantic need forced all consideration of the consequences from his brain. He only knew that he could no longer resist her.

Coming to his feet, he stood before her and tugged his shirt over his head. When he reached for the snap on his fly, Andrea stopped him with a gentle hand. "Let me do it. You didn't give me the opportunity last time. In fact, I recall we didn't completely remove our clothes."

"True, but we were in a hurry."

She slid his zipper down slowly. "Not tonight."

When she had him completely undressed, they continued to stare at each other in the muted light until Sam could stand it no longer. He reached for her and she moved easily into his embrace. He held her a long while, relishing the soft feel of her bare skin against his raging body. Then he kissed her with all the yearning he felt in his soul, with all the need he had harbored since that final moment they were together seven years ago.

The kiss born of emotion soon turned to a kiss of sheer desire. Andrea pressed harder against him, meeting his tongue thrust for blessed thrust. Determined to show her more pleasure, he broke the kiss and settled his lips on her delicate throat then worked his way downward.

She sighed as he plied her breasts with tender kisses. She whimpered as he bent and traced a damp path down her belly with his tongue. She moaned as he fell to his knees and took her with his mouth.

With her hands gripped tightly in his hair, she swayed slightly as he explored the soft folds with his tongue, holding fast to her hips to steady her. But with every sound that escaped her lips, every tremor that ran through her body, he, too, began to feel unsteady. When she tensed and her breathing halted, Sam slipped a finger inside her to prolong her climax, to experience with his own hands the pleasure she now enjoyed.

As her knees began to buckle, he pulled her down onto the blanket and rocked her gently until she seemed to calm.

"That was—" she drew in a broken breath "—remarkable."

He stroked her hair and pressed a kiss against her forehead. "I very much wanted to do that the first time we were together."

"Why didn't you?" she asked, her words muffled against his shoulder.

"I did not want to overwhelm you."

She laughed softly. "I would have definitely been overwhelmed." Pulling away from him, she nudged his chest. "Lie back."

He complied, no longer able to withstand even her slightest command. She set a course down his body with her warm lips, driving him insane with desire when he realized what she intended.

As she reached the plane of his belly below his navel, he laid a hand on her silky hair. "This is not necessary, Andrea."

She raised her head and showed him a determined look. "For me it is. But just so you know, I've never done this before, so you'll have to be patient."

That pleased Sam, knowing she had not had such intimacy with another man. It also forced every thought from his mind when she took him into the silken heat of her mouth and tested its limits. Perhaps she had no experience, but Sam would be hard-pressed to believe that at the moment. She was handling the challenge quite well. He only wished he could say the same for himself.

Nearing the edge, he pulled her head up and kissed her once more. Then he rolled her over and poised himself to enter her. But before he could sink into her, she said, "No."

Sam sighed. "Have you suddenly changed your mind?"

"I've almost lost my mind. We're forgetting something. Again. As much as I love Chance, I don't think it's a good idea to give him a brother or sister."

Sam rolled onto his back, laid an arm over his eyes and cursed his stupidity. How could he be so careless a second time? How could he almost disregard something so very important? Because his only thoughts were of Andrea and making love to her.

"I'll take care of it," she said in a whisper, and before he realized she had moved, he felt her sheath him. "It's okay now," she said quietly.

Sam removed his arm and found her staring at him expectantly, waiting for him to take the next step. He vowed he would not disappoint her.

When Sam pulled Andi back into his arms, she experienced a rush of anticipation. Everything in her life seemed to have come down to this one moment, this reunion of bodies and souls with this one man.

He rolled her to her back and nudged her legs apart with his leg, then entered her with an easy thrust. She had a strong sense of being where she belonged, so close to this man who had lived within her heart for almost a decade.

He moved once more and seated himself deep inside her. A steady moan climbed up her throat and slipped out between her parted lips.

Sam stilled against her. "Have I hurt you?"

"Not in the least." Not yet. But he would when he left again.

"Good. You feel better than I remember," he said with a soft kiss on her brow, his voice strained with his effort to speak.

"So do you," she said, then tilted her hips up to take him completely inside her body. As he set a steady rhythm, she tried to memorize the moments, every incredible sensation, Sam's face as it showed the tension of a man trying to maintain control. How she could relate to that. Right now the bliss of this union was almost more than she could bear without giving in to tears of elation.

"Come with me," Sam murmured, then pulled her over so they faced each other, her leg draped over his hip, their eyes connected as well as their bodies.

"I'm with you," she whispered, and she was. At least for now.

Never in all her imaginings did she ever believe this would happen again. Never did she think that Sam would be making love to her once more, touching her inside and out, drawing another incredible climax from her as he quickened the pace.

She clung to his solid shoulders, held on as if to never let him go. He whispered to her softly in both English and Arabic, heightening the erotic quality of the night and this act. And with one final thrust, he said her name over and over as she relished his climax as well as her own.

The night sounds surrounding them seemed to stop, or maybe it was only Andi's imagination. But she hadn't imagined Sam, the power of his body, the gentleness of his touch, the way he had loved her as if she did mean something to him.

She turned onto her back, breaking the intimate connection between them. She needed to regroup, assess what had happened to her resolve to avoid any emotional entanglement.

How could she have been such an idiot? How could she have believed that by letting him back inside her body, she'd push him out of her heart when she had only drawn him further in?

Sam came up on one bent elbow and braced his cheek on his palm as she stared at the night sky. "Have I disappointed you, Andrea?"

She glanced at him and smiled, though she felt like crying. "No. Not at all." If only he had disappointed her, then she wouldn't be facing such a predicament.

"Perhaps you are wishing on stars again?"

She sighed. "I don't do that anymore, Sam." She had learned long ago that nothing could be gained by such a frivolous activity. She was in charge of her destiny now, at least where Sam was concerned. No matter how wonderful the experience had been, she needed to stay grounded and remember this was only a temporary thing between her and the prince. She couldn't do that with her head off somewhere in the galaxy.

He drew lazy circles around her breasts, and darned if she wasn't reacting as if he had yet to touch her. "Do you not have dreams any longer?"

Oh, she had them. She just refused to buy in to any

of them that dealt with what could never be. "I want to be the best horse trainer the racing world has ever known."

"Much like your father?"

"Daddy was good at what he did, but he never aspired to be the best," Andi replied, more than willing to discuss anything except what had just happened.

"People will know that you are the best," he said adamantly.

She released a humorless laugh. "If you say so."

"They will if I have a say in the matter."

Her gaze zipped to his, fueled by a burst of pride and a spear of anger. "I can do it on my own, Sam. I have to make a name for myself, by myself. It's the only way I'll earn it."

"And you will not accept my help?"

"You've already done enough by letting me train your filly."

"She is yours when I leave, Andrea."

Great. A consolation prize. "You don't have to do that."

"I already have, and I will arrange—at my expense—for her to race when you feel she is ready."

"If you insist that she stay here, I'd like her to belong to Chance."

"As you wish."

Sitting up, she reached for her discarded clothes and began to dress again, before she told him that she loved the horse but she loved him more. Before she did something really crazy like beg him to stay.

"Where are you going?" he asked.

"I imagine Tess is wondering where we are."

"I imagine she has already retired to bed, considering the late hour."

Andi slipped on her panties and shorts then stood. Seeing Sam stretched out on his back still gloriously naked, his dark skin contrasting with the pale-blue blanket, made Andi almost reconsider her departure. But she had to regain her emotional bearings.

Bending down, she retrieved his shorts and tossed them at him. "Put these on, Your Highness. Tess doesn't take too kindly to naked men in her kitchen."

His grin lit up the night. "How do we know that she has not had a naked man in her kitchen?"

Andi groaned. "I don't even want to go there." She thought about what Tess had told her the day before. "I guess you probably know that she and Riley are finally getting married."

"Actually, no."

That surprised Andi. Tess had been an open book since Sam's reappearance. "Well, they are in a few weeks." She sighed. "I can't even imagine Tess being away from the farm."

"They will not live here?" Sam asked.

"They plan on traveling the country."

"You will miss her terribly," he said, a simple statement of fact.

"Of course I will. So will Chance. But we'll manage," she said, although she wasn't sure how. Yet somehow she had always managed the losses in her life, only this time she would feel truly abandoned, especially after Sam left.

"Perhaps you would like me to turn your thoughts to more pleasant things," he said, as if he had somehow tuned in to her mind. Before she could prepare, he tugged her back down against him, amazed to find he was already aroused. And she was more than willing to forget all the sadness, all the tough times to come, in his welcoming arms.

"You're not going to tickle me, are you?" she asked with mock exasperation.

"Not in the way you might imagine, but I'm certain I will find some means to make you feel better."

When he nuzzled her neck, she said, "A good prince is hard to find," feeling lightheaded and lighthearted in his arms. "Or maybe it is the other way around."

"Perhaps we should find out."

Once again Andi's clothes ended up on the nearby grass. And in very little time, Sam had her clinging and gasping and praising his skill.

Too much, she thought as he guided her back to a paradise of his own making. Too little.

Never enough.

Sam stood over Andrea and watched her while she continued to sleep completely unaware he was keeping vigil. He'd been up for hours, had already tended to the horses since he had decided to allow her the luxury of spending extra time in bed. After last night she deserved the added rest.

Silently he admonished himself for his weakness. Scolded himself for not feeling as guilty as he should after making love to her well into the early hours of the morning. Yet he had no regrets except one—their time together was limited.

Seating himself on the edge of the bed, he continued to observe Andrea lying on her belly, still beautifully naked and his to behold a few moments longer. He recalled each and every detail of the night before, unearthed all the feelings for her that should be buried with the past. Yet they were not, nor would they ever be even if miles once again separated him from her.

He glanced at his watch and noted the time. Now nearing 10:00 a.m., he thought it best to wake her or, no doubt, suffer her wrath. Moving closer, he traced his finger down the curve of her spine and onto her buttock. She stirred a little and a sleepy sigh escaped her lips. But he couldn't discern if her eyes had opened, since her hair covered her face in a tangled disarray to match the twisted sheets.

She finally lifted her head, pushed her hair back and regarded him over one shoulder. "What time is it?"

"Time for you to be up and about, I'm afraid."

She rolled onto her back without concern for her nudity. Sam, on the other hand, was very concerned, considering what she was doing to him at that moment. What she had been doing to him since the day of his return.

After glancing at the clock, she sat up with a start. "My gosh, I've wasted most of the day."

"You needed your sleep."

Blessedly she smiled. "I guess so, considering I was up most of the night, thanks to you."

He leaned and kissed her softly on the lips. "No. Many thanks to you."

She stretched and draped her arms around his neck. "I think I used parts of my body that I haven't used in years."

"Then you are in pain?"

"Nice pain. Very nice."

Unable to help himself, he kissed her throat and couldn't resist kissing her breasts. "Perhaps I should do something to alleviate that pain."

"Sorry. We don't have time for that now," she said, then bolted out of the bed, leaving Sam alone to deal with his own discomfort and the emotional wall she had seemed to raise.

After slipping on her robe, she faced him. "I have to put Sunny through some more ground work if I'm going to have her saddled by the end of the month."

Just as well, he decided. If he had his way, they would stay in bed all day without regard for their responsibilities. How easy that would be, now that he had rediscovered the pleasure of making love with Andrea. But he could not disregard what he had to do, not only today but also in a matter of weeks, as much as he would like to forget what awaited him at home. "Riley is in the barn. He's agreed to assist me in making it more serviceable."

She grabbed a brush from the dresser and ran it through her hair with a vengeance. "I can't afford to pay Riley."

"I will see to that."

Tossing the brush aside, she simply said, "Fine, I'm heading to the shower," then left through the door.

Sam was shocked she had not protested his financial offer. Perhaps she was finally beginning to see that his money could only aid in her future and that of their son's.

When he again returned to the stable a few moments later, he discovered that Riley had almost finished removing the old bedding from the first stall in preparation to replace the rubber matting beneath.

Riley looked up and leaned against his shovel, then stroked his too-long mustache. ''Andi still sawin' logs?''

Sam frowned. ''She is awake at the moment.''

He chuckled and scooped another shovelful of bedding into the wheelbarrow. ''I forget you don't always understand the language. Guess it's because I remember the way it used to be when Paul was still around. You were more loose back then. Relaxed. Even the way you talked.''

That was before he had carried the weight of a kingdom on his shoulders. ''I have been away for a long time.''

An uncomfortable silence hung between them until Riley spoke again. ''Did Andi tell you about me and Tess deciding to get hitched?''

''Yes. Last night. Congratulations to you both.''

''Tess told me you're about to do the same come end of the summer.''

''It has been arranged.''

''That's a strange way of putting it.''

Sam saw it exactly as it was, an arrangement. No emotional ties. No vows of love. ''I prefer you not speak of this to Andrea until I have a chance to inform her.''

Riley lifted one shoulder in a shrug. ''That's your business, I guess, but I'm thinkin' she deserves to know.'' He appeared to go back to work, but before Sam could leave to gather more wood to brace the stalls, Riley stopped his departure. ''You know, Andi's dad was a good friend of mine.''

Sam paused and faced the open stall once more. "I remember." He wondered where the conversation might be leading, yet he suspected it would come in the form of a lecture.

"I think he would've liked you a lot."

Sam had not bargained for that presumption. "It is my understanding he was a very good man."

"The best. And he thought the sun rose and set in Andi. Now, I'm not saying he didn't love the boy because he did. But Paulie was more like his mother than Bob—into book learning and that sort of thing." Riley smiled. "Andi was just like her dad, and the apple of his eye. According to him, she could do no wrong."

Sam greatly related to that. "She is a good woman."

"Yep, which is why I have to say something to you."

Exactly as Sam suspected. "I am listening."

Riley raked off his cap and forked a hand through his silver hair, then shoved it back on his head. "Chance is a good kid. He deserves the best. He deserves a dad like Andi's. I've tried to be there for him, to teach him what I know and that ain't too much. But I'm too old to keep up, which is why I'm telling you that if you can't fill those shoes, then maybe you should consider stepping aside to let Andi find someone who can be there for him all the time."

Sam silently cursed Riley's interference, but he understood that it came out of protectiveness for Andrea and Chance. He also realized there was much logic in his assertions. "I will consider your advice."

"That's good. But I also know how hard it is to

ignore a woman like Andi. Tess is much the same. Strong-willed, hard-headed, wild but in some real nice ways. It's not easy to let that kind of woman go.''

Yet that's exactly what Sam had to do—let her go. He'd known that all along. He had known getting involved with her again would be a grave mistake. But he *had* become involved, and now he would have to deal with severing their emotional ties when the time came.

''I promise that whatever I decide to do about my son, it will be best for all concerned.''

''I'm counting on that, Sam.'' Riley set the shovel aside and wiped his hands on his jeans. ''I've got to go do a few things back at the Hammonds' place, but I'll be back at sundown.''

''I will try to finish this stall before you return.''

''You do that.''

Sam stepped aside and allowed him to exit, but before he reached the open door, Riley turned once again. ''And one more thing, Sam. Since I was Andi's dad's best friend, I want you to know that I'm standing in for him.'' He pointed a crooked finger. ''And if you hurt her, you'll have to answer to me.''

With that he was gone, leaving Sam to ponder his words. He had no intention of hurting Andrea, if he could avoid it. But the closer they became, the more the risk increased that he again would shatter her heart. And most likely do a great deal of damage to his own.

Seven

After lunch Sam headed to the stable to resume the repairs. Andrea had only made a brief appearance in the house, grabbed a sandwich then returned to work the horses in the round pen, barely acknowledging him or her aunt.

As Sam neared the barn, he noted the red truck belonging to the man named Caleb parked in the drive. He approached the entrance slowly as he heard the sound of Andrea's laughter, pausing outside to listen. He acknowledged that he had no right to intrude, yet he couldn't stop his eavesdropping.

"Dinner would be great," Andrea said. "But it will have to be in a couple of weeks. Chance will be home and my guest should be leaving."

Her guest? Sam experienced a pang of anger that she considered him only a guest, then admonished himself for such foolishness. He was a guest, not a member of the family. Only a friend, a stranger to his son. Her lover for the time they had remaining, if he had any say in the matter.

That thought sent him forward, but he hesitated once more when the man began to speak. "I'll give you a call next week, unless you decide you want to get together sooner."

Sam could only imagine what this Caleb had in mind for Andrea, and he couldn't contain the spear of jealousy hurling through him. That jealousy thrust him into the barn to find Andrea and Caleb facing each other at the stall containing the filly.

Andrea turned and met Sam's gaze, then smiled. "Speak of the devil, here he is now." She gestured toward him. "Caleb, this is Sam, a family friend."

Sam reluctantly accepted the handshake offered by the cowboy but did not return his smile.

"Nice to meet you, Sam," Caleb said. "Andi tells me you're some kind of a prince."

"A sheikh," he said as politely as his current mood allowed.

"That's great." He gave his grin to Andrea. "Keep up the good work, Andi. I'm pretty pleased with you so far."

Sam wondered what other pleasure he had in mind for Andrea. Forcing the thoughts away, he moved aside and gladly let the man take his leave.

When they were alone once again, Sam lost the tenuous grasp he'd placed on his control. "You will be dining with him after I leave?"

Andrea picked up a plastic box containing supplies and walked into the tack room. "Looks that way."

Propelled by his insane envy, Sam followed her inside. "Will Chance be in attendance?"

"Yes," she answered curtly.

"Does our son like this man?"

"He's not been around him all that much."

"Then you have no way of knowing if this Caleb will be an acceptable suitor."

Andi dropped the box at her feet and turned, leaning against the saddle set atop the stand. "I personally don't think Caleb is an appropriate suitor, because he's married and has two kids."

"He has a wife?"

"Yes, he has a wife, and she'll be coming with us. Are you satisfied now?"

Sam was still reluctant to trust the man. "I'm admittedly concerned about his motives regardless of his marital status."

Andrea rolled her eyes to the ceiling, then turned her back and began oiling the saddle. "Look, Sam, Caleb is a nice guy. He's really done me a favor by letting me train his horse, and that's the only thing he's asked of me."

"To this point."

She faced him, twisting the rag in her fist. "I don't know why you keep thinking he has other things in mind. You don't even know him."

He knew his type, and he knew how tempting Andrea could be. She was tempting him greatly now with the fire in her eyes and the clothes she wore, a sleeveless rag of a shirt cut short at her midriff, giving him a glimpse of her navel, where her jeans rode low at her shapely hips. The cowboy might be wed but he was still a man. And Sam had no right to judge anyone, considering what he had done with Andrea last night, knowing he was bound to another. Considering that he had not yet had his fill of her, as if he ever would.

"I will not mention it again," he conceded, though he knew he would think about it often in the days to come, as well as when he returned to Barak. He would think about her often, wondering if she would find her way to another man's arms, another man's bed.

But until that time she was his, and although it would be inadvisable to pursue a physical relationship with her, he was not strong enough to resist. He had no intention of resisting. If all he could have was a few stolen moments, then so be it.

Sam could only stare at Andrea as she cleaned the saddle, bending down now and then to retrieve supplies for the task. His body raged with need when the denim pulled tight over her hips, revealing the shape of her buttocks. Her hair was secured and bound high on her head in a band, leaving the back of her slender neck fair game. Sam imagined kissing her there. Kissing her everywhere.

"Do you need my assistance?" he asked.

She sent him a coy look over her shoulder. "I've cleaned so many saddles I could probably do it blindfolded."

"I assume you could do many things blindfolded."

Andi froze with her hand midswipe when she felt the heat of Sam's body at her back. A pleasant tremor crept up her spine as he tugged the bandanna from her back pocket then snaked it across her shoulder and over one breast before drawing it up slowly.

"Should we see if it is true that you are skilled without the benefit of sight?" His voice was a warm, midnight breeze at her ear.

Before she could respond, he placed the cloth over her eyes and tied it, throwing her into darkness, throwing her body into a carnal tailspin.

"You're really going to make me clean the saddle blindfolded?" she asked, her voice little more than a croak, knowing that's not what he'd meant at all.

Taking her by the shoulders, he turned her around and nudged her back against the saddle. "I propose that we ignore the saddle for more pleasant endeavors." He softly kissed her with an added sweep of his tongue across her lower lip. "I want you to concentrate on what I am doing to you."

A wave of heat ignited low in her belly then alighted between her thighs. "I've been working, Sam. I'm hot and sweaty." A feeble protest that she hoped he would ignore.

"So am I," he said. "But my hands are clean."

His hands were wonderful as he skimmed them down her sides, grazing her breasts. "What about Tess?" She worried they might get caught, yet that prospect heightened her desire.

"Tess has gone to the market," he whispered as he laved his tongue over her earlobe. "Riley will not return until sundown."

When she clutched his arms to secure herself, he pulled her hands away and held them at her sides. "Do not touch me yet," he said.

Andi gripped the metal stand to remain upright when her knees threatened to give way. She stood and waited for the longest moment until Sam caught her hands once more and placed a kiss on each palm before resting them against his face.

"Touch me now, Andrea. Remember me."

How could she ever forget him? Heavens, she had tried, but without success. She was tired of trying.

On that thought, she explored his wonderful face with her hands, a face that had invaded her dreams in great detail so many nights before—details deeply engrained in her memory and her heart. She traced a finger over the strong plane of his nose, the bow of his beautiful, full mouth, the solid jaw covered by a spattering of whiskers. It didn't matter that she couldn't see him now—he would always be with her, branded into her brain.

Gliding her hands down the column of his throat, she continued on to his chest, pausing when she realized he had removed his shirt, much to her delight. His skin was damp and hot beneath her palms as she set a course across the crisp hair and on to his nipples that peaked into tiny pebbles beneath her fingertips. She traveled down his abdomen, and his muscles clenched when she circled a finger in his navel. Intending to continue her erotic exploration, she slipped her fingertips beneath the band of his jeans, only to have him stop her as he gripped her wrist.

"Raise your arms," he said.

As if a master puppeteer was controlling her, she complied, leaning back against the saddle for support while he tugged her shirt over her head, leaving her completely naked from the waist up. He ran a fingertip across her chest from shoulder to shoulder, much the same as she had done to him. He traced her breasts with sensuous strokes of his fingertips, with agonizing slowness as he decreased the circles when he reached her nipples.

"You are very beautiful in the daylight," he said in a deep, slow-burn voice that complemented his avid touch.

"This isn't fair," she said on a broken breath. "You can see me but I can't see you."

"You only need to feel at the moment."

No problem, Andi thought as the heat of his mouth engulfed her nipple. She bucked at the pleasurable sensations, giving everything over to feeling. He paid equal attention to both breasts as she molded her hands to his scalp and followed his movements. Then suddenly he raised his head and commanded, "Turn around."

She did as she was told, bracing her hands on the saddle to regain her ground. Sam tracked his way down her spine, first with his thumbs then with his lips, leaving a trail of wonderful chills in his wake. Tuned in solely to Sam's sensual torture, it took Andi a moment to realize he had slipped one hand between her and the saddle. She felt the downward track of her zipper and went weak with anticipation, and weaker still when he lowered the denim to her thighs, taking her panties with it. A wisp of warm air whisked over her now-exposed bottom, but it was nothing compared to the heat Sam generated as he pressed more kisses to her lower back, then kissed her bottom.

Andi lowered her chin to her chest, savoring the feel of his mouth, gasping at the tiny nip of his teeth that he soothed with his tongue.

"A very nice dessert," he added with a low chuckle that sounded from deep within his chest.

She couldn't argue that point. This was much better than a hot-fudge sundae with whipped cream and nuts. Better than anything she had imagined to this point.

After working his way back up, he cupped his palm between her thighs while feathering kisses across the back of her neck, yet he only toyed with the cover of curls. Overcome with the need for him to pacify the insistent throbbing, she pressed against his hand in encouragement.

Andi couldn't stifle the moan of frustration when he took his touch away. "Patience," he scolded. "I will see to your needs but first I must see to something else."

When she heard the sound of his zipper followed by the rattle of paper, Andi realized that Sam had planned this all along. Planned to make her mindless with wanting despite his initial opposition. And more important, he was ruining her for other men. Convincing her with every kiss, every touch, that no one would ever measure up to him. But she really didn't care. She only cared about right now, the absolute need, the undeniable ache that could only be relieved by this particular prince.

He was soon flush against her back, returning his hand to the place that wept for his attention. This time he delved into the damp folds until he found her center to caress and cajole with firm yet tender fingertips. She was soon caught up in a whirlwind of sensory details surrounding her—freshly cut hay, mingled with the scent of leather and Sam. She heard his shallow breathing and the sounds of horses chomping their hay. But all sounds, all smells disappeared as he fondled her straight into oblivion.

The climax began to build and build, and she only knew that she wanted him inside her *now*. Reaching back to grasp his hips, she pulled him forward, and he entered in one sharp, enthralling thrust, bringing about an earth-moving climax.

She turned her face toward him and accepted his deep, penetrating kiss. His tongue captured the rhythm of his body as he explored her eager mouth while he moved inside her, stifling her gasps as he filled her completely.

He continued to stroke her even after her release had subsided. "Again, Andrea."

"I'm not sure—"

"I am," he insisted. "You will."

Amazingly, she did, moments before Sam found his own release. He gripped her hips, and a steady groan escaped his mouth as she absorbed the weight of his body against hers. Burying his face between her shoulder blades, he held her tightly. She couldn't tell who was shaking more, him or her. They were so close it was hard to tell where one began and the other ended. So close that Andi wanted to stay this way forever.

"You take me to limits I have never known before," he whispered. "I have never known anything such as this."

Neither had Andi. And she would probably never know anything like it again.

Reality took hold when she suddenly realized that someone had pulled up into the drive. And, considering the familiar sound of the noisy tailpipe, she knew exactly who that someone might be.

"Tess!"

Shoving Sam away with a push of her hips, she yanked the bandanna from her eyes and pulled her pants back up. She fumbled for her shirt, now covered in sawdust and straw, and pulled it over her head.

Awareness finally hit Sam but he seemed in no hurry. "Get dressed," Andi hissed. "She might come in here."

"I assume she would put away the groceries first," he said, taking his sweet time redoing his jeans.

She shoved his shirt at him. "Your assumptions could be wrong, and we'd have the devil to pay."

He had the gall to grin.

Sam Yaman was much too confident, Andi decided. Too practiced in his efficiency, she thought, when he calmly tossed the condom and package into the trash bin then covered it with a feed sack.

He turned his deadly grin back on her. "All evidence has been disposed of, and no one will know what deeds have been done in this room."

Andi glanced down at her disheveled clothes and could only imagine how she would look to her aunt. "Guess I could tell Tess that we had an unexpected tornado come through the barn."

He kicked the door closed, taking Andi by surprise. "We could lock out the world and stay in here the remainder of the afternoon." He stalked toward her and pulled her into his arms. "After all, we still have much to learn about each other."

"I'd be willing to spend a lifetime having you teach me."

His expression went serious. "If only that were possible."

Suddenly chilled, she backed out of his embrace. "Don't look so worried, Sam. I told you I don't expect anything. I was just spouting off."

"You have no idea how much I wish that we could be together." Her heart soared, then fell once again when he declared, "But that is not possible."

She propped a hand on her hip and glared at him. "I've always believed that anything's possible."

"Not in this instance, Andrea."

She forced back the unexpected tears burning hot behind her eyes. "Why? Because of your duty? Don't you realize you could be happy here with us? I've seen your happiness, Sam. You smile more now. You're enjoying yourself, especially with Chance. You might as well be wearing a blindfold if you don't see it, too."

He kicked the barrel containing the feed, causing a loud thump that would surely give them away if anyone were nearby. "Of course I am happy here. I have always been happy here. But that does not change my circumstance. I have to see to my obligations."

How many more times would she have to hear this? "Obligations to whom? Your father?"

"To my…" He looked away. "Yes, to my father. To my people."

Andi swiped away one rogue tear. "Well, great. I guess that doesn't include your son." *Or me.*

"I have told you I will provide—"

"Money. I know. But that won't buy you his love, Sam. Your money and your station won't buy you happiness, either."

Without a word he yanked open the door and left Andi alone with her sorrow once more. If only he knew how much she loved him. If only he would consider the possibilities. But something was keeping him from doing that, and she wondered if there was more to his resistance than his duty. Something he was failing to tell her.

She intended to find out the sheikh's secrets, even if it was the last thing she did before he left.

Sam spent the coming days working on the stable with Riley, but he spent the nights in Andrea's arms. She had proved to be an uninhibited lover, wild in the ways that she pleased him. Each time they were together, he discovered something new about her, acknowledged that she was forever imbedded in his soul.

He engaged in a constant battle between guilt and desire, love and responsibility. His desire and love for Andrea had won out, at least for now. When he took Maila as his wife—if he took her as his wife—he was sentencing himself to a loveless union. And when he took her to his bed, he would forever imagine Andrea.

That would be doing a grave disservice to Maila. She was a good woman who deserved a man who could give more of himself. An educated woman who, like him, agreed to the union out of a sense of obligation to their families. Yet if Sam ended the arrangement, in doing so he would encounter his father's scorn.

He would have to decide what would be best for everyone involved, a decision that would not come easily. And in a scarce few days, he would be leaving his son, and Andrea.

After his shower, he walked downstairs to find Andrea on the phone. She worried her bottom lip as she spoke quietly. "Okay, sweetie. You sleep tight now, and I'll see you tomorrow."

Sam seated himself on the sofa and gestured for Andrea to join him after she replaced the phone in its cradle. The concern in her expression could not be denied, even when she smiled at him.

"That was Chance," she said. "He wanted to make sure we're going to pick him up in the limo."

Sam returned her smile to mask his own worry. "And you assured him that we would?"

"Yes."

Sam patted the seat beside him. "Come tell me what is troubling you."

Instead of taking her place next to him, she curled into his lap. He held her tightly, savoring the scent of her shower-damp hair and the softness of her fragile body encased in satin.

"I'm worried about Chance," she said.

"Is he not well?"

She glanced up at him, then tucked her head beneath his chin. "He says he's fine, but he sounds tired."

"I would assume he is tired."

"I hope that's all it is."

He brushed a kiss over her forehead and stroked her hair. "What would lead you to believe otherwise?"

"Mother's intuition. Or maybe I'm just being paranoid like always."

"You are only concerned for his well-being, Andrea."

She sighed. "I know. But when he was almost three, he climbed up on a fence rung and fell backward. He seemed to be okay, but then the next morning he complained about his shoulder. I took him to the doctor and found out he'd broken his collarbone. I should've taken him that night."

Sam tipped her chin up, forcing her to look at him. "It was a simple mistake, Andrea. It does not mean that you don't care for him."

"I realize that, but I felt horrible, like a bad mother."

"You are a wonderful mother," Sam said adamantly. "I could not have picked a better mother for my child."

She touched her lips to his cheek, stirring his body and his soul. "Thanks." After studying him a long moment, she said, "Now tell me what's bugging you."

Sam should be surprised that she so easily saw through him, but he wasn't. It seemed that over the past week they had become totally tuned in to each other's moods, each other's needs. Perhaps it had always been that way. Perhaps it always would.

"I'm afraid I have some less-than-satisfactory news."

Andrea's frame stiffened in his arms. "What is it?"

"I spoke with my father earlier today. I must return to Barak on Thursday."

"You weren't supposed to leave until Sunday." She stared at him with fire and frustration in her eyes.

"So he snaps his fingers and you come running. Wish I knew his secret."

"It is complicated, Andrea. I do not have the luxury of coming and going as I please."

She slid off his lap and claimed the place at the end of the sofa. "I'm sorry for you, Sam. It must be awful to have that kind of burden, to not have free will."

Anger gripped Sam and he struggled to temper his fury. "I have free will. I also have responsibilities."

She rolled her eyes to the ceiling. "I know, I know. But what about your responsibility to your child? You've barely spent any time with him. Is this what he'll have to count on in the future, a father who may or may not come to see him?"

Sam sat forward and lowered his head. "I have been considering that. I can only promise that I will try to be here as much as possible."

Andrea sighed. "We don't have much time to decide when to tell him, do we?"

They had little time to be together, as well. "No, we do not."

Andrea rose from the sofa. "Guess we'll cross that bridge when we come to it."

Sam stood. "What time will we leave tomorrow morning to pick up Chance?"

She folded her arms across her breasts and faced him. "Not we, Sam. You."

He frowned. "I do not understand."

"I've decided *you* should pick him up by yourself. That way you can have time alone with him to get to know him."

"But you—"

"I'll see him when you get back. Besides, I'll have him with me for the rest of my life. You, on the other hand, have very little time."

Sam realized the difficulty of her decision and the heartache he was causing her. "Are you certain this is what you want?"

"Yes, I'm sure."

"Do you wish me to tell him—"

"No, I don't want you to say anything about you being his father. I think I should be there."

"I will honor your request."

She started toward the stairs. "Good night, Sam."

"I will join you in a few moments."

She turned to him once again. "I'd like to sleep alone tonight. I'm exhausted."

In her own way she was already preparing to let him go, that much Sam knew. "I will do what you ask, Andrea, but I would like to spend this last night with you, before Chance returns."

"It's okay, Sam," she said in a weary tone. "We've both known all along this wasn't forever. Might as well end it now."

He wanted to shout that he wanted no part of this ending, that he wanted to forever be by her side, in her bed, in her life. Instead he turned his back and said, "I wish you pleasant dreams, Andrea."

Her sharp, mirthless laugh stopped him cold. "I don't believe in dreams, Sam. Not anymore."

Eight

"**W**here on earth are they?" Andi paced the length of the kitchen as she stared at the clock that read 3:00 p.m. Long past time for Sam and Chance's arrival home from the camp.

"Maybe they stopped off for some lunch," Tess offered as she poured her and Riley another glass of tea at the table.

"I packed them a lunch," Andi responded, unable to keep the panic from her voice. "I wanted to make sure Chance has the right things to eat."

"I'm sure they just stopped off for a picnic, then," Riley said. "Sam seems like a fairly responsible guy."

Andi spun around to face the pair. "Yeah, that's how he seems, but how well do we really know him?"

Tess frowned. "Andi, you're talking nonsense. This is Sam, the boy who practically lived here for four years. The same one who worked on the barn for the past two weeks like some hired hand."

"He's changed, Tess. He's not the same. What if he's decided to go to the airport and just keep going from there? What if he takes Chance back to his country?"

Tess rose from the kitchen table and took Andi by both arms. "Just listen to yourself, Andi. You're not making any sense. Sam promised he wouldn't try something like that."

"He promised a lot of things, Tess, and he didn't keep those promises, either. How can I trust that he won't do the same thing again?"

Tess narrowed her eyes and studied Andi dead-on. "Trust your heart, Andi."

Andi didn't dare. She'd done that before only to be crushed in the process.

The shrill of the phone caused Andi to jump. Pushing away from Tess, she grabbed it on the second ring. "Hello?"

"Could I please speak to Ms. Andrea Hamilton," a soft feminine voice asked.

Frustrated that it wasn't Sam, Andrea sighed. She didn't need home repairs or a magazine subscription. "That depends on who you are."

"I'm Mrs. Murphy with the hospital in Lexington, and I'm calling concerning your son."

Sheer panic pierced through Andi's momentary shock. "Has there been an accident?"

Tess quickly came to Andi's side as the woman

continued to speak. "No, no accident. A Mr. Yaman brought Chance in. The boy's blood sugar is low."

"Is he okay?"

"He's in the E.R. being examined now. Mr. Yaman asked if I would notify you."

"I'm on my way." Andi hung up without saying goodbye and grabbed her keys from the hook by the back door. "Chance is at the hospital," she called to Tess on her way out.

"Let me drive you, Andi," Tess said at the door while Andi crossed the yard to the pickup.

"I'll call you."

"Andi, are you sure?"

She dismissed Tess with a wave. "I'm fine."

But was Chance?

Andi managed the thirty-mile drive in record time. She rushed into the emergency room barking inquiries to anyone who would listen. Finally one nurse directed her to a curtained cubicle down a narrow corridor.

Stepping inside, Andi stopped short at the scene playing out before her. Among the all-too-familiar sterile scents and scenery, Sam was stretched out in the small hospital bed, Chance curled against his side with his face turned in profile as his head rested against his father's solid chest.

Andi covered her mouth to stifle a sob when she caught sight of the IV tubing trailing from Chance's slender arm. But she couldn't hold back the emotions when she noted how natural they looked—one beautiful man with his large hand enfolding the equally beautiful child's smaller one, an overt display of protection. The identical dark hair, the dark lashes fanned against their cheeks as they slept, presented a picture of peace that starkly contrasted with the colorless surroundings.

As Andi took another step forward, Sam's eyes snapped opened and he attempted a smile. Quietly he slipped his arm from beneath Chance and slid out of the bed without disturbing their son. He gestured for Andi to step outside. Reluctantly she complied, torn between wanting to hold her precious child and needing to hear what Sam had to say.

"What happened?" she said, her voice hoarse with fear, clouded with emotions that she tried to keep at bay.

Sam rubbed a hand over his jaw. "On the ride home he became very pale. I offered him some juice, as you'd instructed, but he refused. Then he began to perspire and became agitated. We were nearing Lexington so I instructed Rashid to come here. I knew not what else to do."

"You did the right thing, Sam."

He glanced away but not before Andi glimpsed the worry in his near-black eyes. "I have never feared much in my lifetime, Andrea. But this terrified me." He finally turned his gaze back to her. "I only now realize how much you have been through with this disease."

"What Chance has been through," Andi corrected. "It's something you learn to deal with as a parent of an ill child. My love for him has seen me through."

"I suppose I am only beginning to understand that concept."

Andi bit the inside of her cheek to stop another

onslaught of tears over Sam's obvious pain. She had to stay composed. "Has the doctor seen him?"

"Yes, a few minutes ago. He said that his levels seem to be stable, but he would like him to stay for a few hours to be certain."

Andi drew in a slow breath of relief and released it on a shaky sigh. "That's routine."

"Then he has suffered this before?"

"Yes. Several times at first, but not in a while."

"The doctor believes that Chance's exhaustion perhaps brought on this attack."

Andi silently cursed her stupidity. "I should never have let him go to camp."

Sam took her by the arm and guided her against the wall opposite the cubicle. "Do not blame yourself, Andrea. Chance told me how much he enjoyed his time at the camp. You had no reason to believe this would happen."

She shot a glance at the parted curtain to see that Chance still slept. "I should've known."

Sam brushed a lock of hair away from her face, damp with the tears she had shed on the ride to Lexington. "The doctor also said you should consider putting Chance on a medicine pump to replace the shots."

"I've wanted to do that," Andi said. "But it's very expensive. I've been trying to save enough money to cover what the insurance won't pay."

"I will take care of it," Sam insisted. "You need not worry about funds."

She was worried about many things at the moment. "Did you tell anyone you're Chance's father?"

"I told the physician, but Chance did not hear me, if that is your concern."

Andi felt incredibly selfish to question him at such a time. "I wasn't worried exactly. I'd just hate to think that Chance learned something so important while he's sick."

"I've told him nothing, even when he asked many questions on the ride back."

Andi's concern came calling again. "What questions?"

"He wanted to know if I knew his father. I told him that I did, but not very well. And that is the truth, Andrea." He streaked a hand over his face. "I realize I don't know myself at all."

Andi laid a hand on his arm. "I know you, Sam. You're a good man. A good father."

He studied her with weary eyes. "Am I, Andrea? I am a father who must leave his son. There is nothing good in that."

"You can enjoy the time you have with him now so he can get to know you as his father."

"Perhaps it would be best if he never knows."

Best for whom? Andi wanted to shout. Best for him, no doubt. No ties except for providing money. No commitment to their son, or to her. "Let's not talk about this here. I need to be with Chance."

"I only wanted you to know that I am considering our son's well-being. If that entails giving him up, I will not hesitate to consider it."

Andi's heart plummeted, causing a painful ache in her chest brought about by an overwhelming sadness. "If that's what you want."

"I promise you, Andrea, it is not what I wish at all. But it could be the best decision for Chance."

Too tired to fight, too heartsick to talk, Andrea walked away to see her son, the only constant in her life.

Sam spent the better part of the week getting to know his son. While looking on with the eye of a concerned parent, he'd taught Chance how to hammer a nail. Yet he felt it necessary to treat the boy as if he had no deficit. On the surface Chance appeared to behave as any normal boy would, active and enthusiastic, embracing life to its fullest. But now that Sam had witnessed the effects of his disease, he worried all the more.

At least Andrea seemed to be very optimistic, now that Chance had begun using a pump that kept the medication flowing into his body. She had told Sam that his levels were much better, and that Chance was much more energetic than before. A very good thing, Sam decided. And he certainly could confirm his son's zeal for activity.

Presently Chance was helping him sweep the aisle between the stalls. With his small hand—a miniature version of Sam's own—poised on the push broom that was almost as tall as the child, he asked, "Do I look like my dad?"

Sam carefully weighed the question. "Yes, to some degree."

"Like how?"

"The color of your skin and your hair. I believe your eyes are lighter in color."

Leaning the broom against one stall, Chance studied his arms then wrinkled his nose. "I've got Mama's freckles."

Sam laughed as he had many times in previous days over his child's antics. "Yes, you do."

Chance toed a pile of hay with one booted foot. "My friend Bobby says that where you live it's nothing but sand."

As Chance had done, Sam propped his broom against the opposite stall. "That is true to a point, we do have quite a bit of sand. But we also have trees and mountains. And a very good university we've built in the last few years as well as an excellent hospital."

Chance frowned. "I hate hospitals."

Sam's first fatherly faux pas. "I'm certain you do, and with good reason. But they are necessary."

"I still hate 'em." Chance turned his eyes to Sam, eyes so very much like his own. "Do all the people look alike in your country?"

"Most have dark skin and features, but they are all very different."

"Are they nice?"

"As it is in America, there are some very good people and some not so good people. There are mothers and fathers, sisters and brothers who play together and argue with each other. Teachers, doctors and builders. Overall, it is a very peaceful place to live."

"Do you live in a palace?"

"Yes. It has been in my family for many generations."

"Can I come visit you sometime?"

Sam's chest tightened with remorse, wishing that were possible. "Perhaps when you are older."

He released a long sigh. "I sure wish you could stay here. Don't you like America?"

"I like it very much. In fact, I was born here, in the state of Ohio."

"Then if you're American, how come you don't live here?"

At times Sam had desired that very thing, now more than ever, but he still had a strong allegiance to his country. Although they had made many strides, there was still much to be done. "I cannot live here because my father is the king of my country and I am to take his place one day."

"Maybe you could call him and tell him to hire someone else to do it." His eyes widened with innocence. "One of the girls at camp said her dad doesn't have a job. Maybe he'd do it."

Sam knelt at Chance's level with a tenderness radiating from his heart over the child's simple logic. "It is very complicated, Chance. I was born to lead my country, to help my people." He brushed a tendril of hair from his forehead. "Do you understand now why I must leave?"

He shrugged. "I guess, but I still wish you would stay." Chance wrapped his frail arms around Sam's neck in an embrace, taking Sam by surprise and his heart by storm. "I still wish you were my dad."

Andi stood outside the barn, frozen in place while awaiting Sam's response to Chance's wish. Yet he only said, "Let us finish our work so we're not late for supper."

She leaned back against the outside wall of the barn, closed her eyes against the setting sun and released a slow uneven breath. He'd had the perfect opportunity to tell Chance. Maybe he was still honoring her request that she be there when the moment arrived. Or maybe Sam was serious about not telling Chance the truth.

That made her incredibly troubled that she would continue to live a lie. If Sam insisted that Chance not know, should she tell him anyway? Maybe when he was much older, then she would make the revelation—and more than likely face his wrath because of her deceit. Would Chance blame her or would he blame Sam? Would he ever understand that his father thought it best? Would he realize that Sam was being unselfish in his decision, and that it had caused him great pain?

"You're looking a little pale, Andi girl. Did you work too hard today?"

Andi opened her eyes to find Tess staring at her inquisitively. She pushed off the wall and folded her arms across her chest. "Sam leaves tomorrow," she said.

Tess patted Andi's shoulder. "I know, honey. And I wanted to talk to you about that very thing."

"I'm going to be okay."

"You will if you do what I tell you to do."

Andi rolled her eyes skyward. "Do I really have to hear this?"

"Yes, you do." Tess forked a hand through her short gray hair. "Tonight I want Chance to come to the bunkhouse and stay with me. That will give you the opportunity to say your goodbyes to Sam, and I want you to do it properly."

"I don't think that's necessary."

Tess sent her a stern look. "Yes, it is. You take tonight and you spend it with him. You make those memories because they'll be all you'll ever have. You keep them in your heart and you bring them out when times are tough."

It sounded simple enough, but past experience had taught Andi it was anything but simple. "I don't need more memories, Tess."

"Yes, you do. I could never have made it without mine all these years."

Andi sported a frown of her own, confused over Tess's veiled revelation. "Does this have to do with you and some man other than Riley?"

Glancing away, Tess muttered, "Yes," then after a pause continued. "It was a long time ago. He was a soldier, a real good-looking fellow, not that I couldn't hold my own back then," she added with a grin. "He asked me to marry him before he left for the war, and I turned him down."

Andi shifted her weight from one hip to the other. "And he didn't ask again when he came home?"

"He never came home."

"Oh, Tess," Andi said, hugging her aunt against her. "I'm so sorry."

"Don't be," Tess said when they parted. "I confess I regret that I didn't say yes, but I regret more that the should-have-beens have kept me from living my life all these years. I don't want that to happen to you."

Andi sighed and pushed back the tears. "It's going to be so hard, letting him go." Harder than the first time. Harder than anything Andi had ever done before.

Tess braced Andi's shoulders and gave her a little shake. "But you have to let him go. You have to for your sake and for your son's. You take tonight and you show him that you love him. Tell him that you love him, because I know you do. If he walks away after that, then it was never meant to be in the first place."

The "give them wings" theory that Andi was coming to despise. But she saw the logic in her aunt's advice, and she made the decision to have one last night with Sam, her lover, the love of her life.

Chance came bounding out of the barn door shouting, "I'm hungry!" interrupting the emotional moment.

Tess caught him on the fly and whirled him around. "You eat as much as a moose these days."

"I am a moose," Chance proclaimed, followed by a high-pitched giggle.

Tess set him on his feet and grinned. "Tell you what, Mr. Moose. Why don't you come spend the night in the bunkhouse with me? Riley's coming over and we can play some checkers."

Chance's expression brightened. "Can Riley teach me how to play poker?"

Both Andi and Tess laughed then. "I guess we can do that, Little Bit," Tess said. "As long as your mama doesn't mind."

Andi pretended to think long and hard before saying, "As long as you don't bet away the house and the horses."

"We'll stick to pennies," Tess said. She turned her attention back to Chance. "Then it's settled. Right after dinner, we'll play some poker."

"Can Sam play, too?" Chance asked.

Tess sent Andi a meaningful glance. "I think Sam has a few things to tend to tonight with your mama."

Sam had longed to tell Chance the truth, yet he hadn't. He had longed to declare that he was the father Chance had wished for, yet he couldn't. If he had made that admission knowing he would leave the next day, never to return, it would have been selfish on his part and totally unfair to his son. And he couldn't return, not after knowing what it would be like to remain a part of this blessed family. Knowing each time it would be more difficult to leave. He could only hope that one day Andrea would find a suitable father for Chance. That consideration made him wince with a pain so deep that it threatened to consume him.

"It is for the best," he kept repeating to himself as he had during dinner, quite possibly the last meal he would ever share with his son or Andrea.

The finality sat heavily on his heart as he began to pack the rest of his belongings. He'd saved the most significant for last—the baseball, Paul's graduation gift to him, even the pair of tattered jeans he had left behind before. All mementos from the past that he would cherish throughout his future. Yet when he opened his suitcase once more, he found lying atop his clothing a souvenir that captured the present.

The photograph was much the same as the one of him, Andi and Paul except Chance had replaced his uncle. Tess had taken it earlier in the week, but he had no idea when she'd had it developed or how it had ended up among his things. Perhaps she had placed it there when he had returned to the stable for one last look after the evening meal. Perhaps it wasn't Tess's doing at all. If his instincts served him correctly, Andrea had left the keepsake, another precious gift she had given him.

Andrea.

He wanted desperately to go to her, to take her in his arms one final time, to spend a few more moments in her presence, to make love to her as he had desired to do the past week. He would deny himself that pleasure for he did not deserve her attention. And more than likely she would refuse if he dared make the offer tonight.

He picked up the photo and studied it a moment longer, admiring the faces of the woman he had always loved, of the child he had grown to love. Tomorrow he would say goodbye to them both and wish them well, then return to his homeland and pretend that nothing had changed. Yet everything had changed, especially Sheikh Samir Yaman.

"It's a nice picture, isn't it?"

His hands froze on the framed photo at the soothing sound of Andrea's voice coming from behind him. After carefully tucking the photo beneath a few garments to protect it, he closed the suitcase and closed the chapter on what could never be.

Slowly he turned to face the woman who had so easily secured his heart years ago. "I will cherish it always," he said. "Thank you."

She took a tentative step forward and stopped at the end of the four-poster bed. "It's the least I could do."

"It is very much appreciated."

As a heavy silence hung between them, she pushed her red-gold hair away from her face but failed to look directly at him. Finally she walked forward and stood face-to-face with him, so close that he could see that her heartache had settled in her beautiful blue eyes. He opened his arms to her, and she moved into his embrace.

Andi settled her cheek against Sam's chest, not certain whose heart was beating more rapidly, his or hers. But her heart was in the process of totally splintering.

On that thought she kissed his whisker-rough jaw and gathered all her courage to tell him the one thing she had avoided until now. "I love you, Sam."

He touched her face with tenderness and gently kissed her brow. "As I love you."

She experienced an overwhelming joy that raced to her soul and settled on her wounded heart. "Then stay with me. Be a part of our lives."

"You know that I cannot do that."

She stared at him in frustration. "Then you don't really love me."

His rough sigh echoed in the silent room. "Yes, I do, more than you will ever know. But that does not change my situation."

"It could if you wanted it to."

"If only that were true." He guided her to the edge of the bed and seated her next to his side, then took her hands into his. "I also love our son, which is why I have decided that he need never know I am his father."

Exactly what she'd feared. "But what about when you come back?"

He glanced away but not before revealing an abiding sadness in his stoic expression. "I will not be coming back."

Andi's heart started another descent. "But you have to come back. Chance needs you. *I* need you."

"You need to resume your life without me. You need to find someone who will care for you and our son. Someone who is deserving of your love."

"I don't want anyone but you," she said, warm tears now raining down her cheeks in a stream of sorrow.

"You say that now, but you will change your mind once I am gone."

He pulled her tightly into his strong arms. If only Andi could absorb some of that strength. If only she could have foreseen where this would lead. In reality she'd known all along what would happen, that he *would* leave her again, but she had chosen to believe that somehow, some way, it would be different this time. That he might actually change his mind, that she would change his mind. How foolish she'd been.

She had no choice but to claim the sadness, to accept defeat. But she didn't know how to accept his leaving. "I don't know how to let you go."

"You must."

She raised her head and looked at him straight-on, determined to try one more time to make him see things her way. "Even if you give up your wealth, your status, just look at what you'd be getting in return."

"How well I know this."

"Then why does it have to be this way? Why do

you have to go? Why? And what is it you're not telling me?''

He remained silent for a moment before drawing in a deep, cleansing breath. ''I am to marry another.''

Nine

Sam had been prepared for Andrea's shock over his sudden announcement. He had not been prepared for the seething anger boiling beneath the surface of her calm facade, apparent from the narrowing of her blue eyes.

"And you've known this all along?" Her tone was surprisingly controlled.

Sam wished she would shout at him. He deserved her hostility, her fury. "Yes, I have, but I must explain what this involves."

She bolted from the bed, away from him. "You are damned right you must explain."

He knew not where to begin, since there seemed to be no excuse for his behavior. "This marriage is an arrangement and nothing more. The details are to be finalized when I return. But rest assured, I do not love her, Andrea."

She wrapped her arms about her middle. "Well, great. That makes me feel a whole lot better."

"I have also decided that I will discuss this marriage with my father on my return. I am considering not going through with it."

She glared at him. "Bully for you."

How could he get through to her? How could he convince her that his heart was solely in her possession? He rose and clasped her slender arms. "I've decided I cannot live that lie, Andrea, not with what I've found with you. Maila is a good woman, and like you she deserves a man who can give all of himself to her."

"When did you figure this out, Sheikh Yaman? Before or after you had sex with me?"

Anger roiled within Sam. "I made love to you, Andrea, and if you recall, at your insistence. I have always been weak in your presence. Always. I have never been able to resist you from the moment that Paul brought me here."

"So it's my fault that you cheated on your fiancée, is it?"

"It is my fault for not being a stronger man."

"So answer this," she said sternly. "If you're getting out of this marriage, then why can't you be with us?"

"Must I remind you again about my status?"

She took a few more steps away from him. "Heavens, no. If I hear that one more time, I'll scream. But it seems to me that you just don't get it. All the finest things in the world will never replace love, Sam. Your son's love. My love. But if your riches and your title mean so much to you, then you're right, it's better that you leave for good.''

With that, she started for the door. Sam quickly came to his feet. "I beg you Andrea, please stay. Let us take this time to talk things through, to be with each other. This last night will be all that we ever have.''

Slowly she turned to face him. "No, Sam, I won't. I'm letting you go, starting now.''

Andrea realized there had been a lot of truth in Sam's words the night before. She had been the one to entice him. She had insisted they make love. Yet he had refused to tell her about his impending marriage, and that not only stung but it angered her, as well.

All that wounded pride and horrible hurt had prevented her from spending more time with him, making more memories. In some ways she'd regretted that decision, but no matter how hard it had been to walk away, she had known that she would only have more trouble seeing him off this morning.

Obviously she had been wrong to trust him. Maybe he didn't really love her. Maybe in reality he viewed her only as a convenience. But he had made love to her so sweetly, and he had told her that he loved her. Regardless of her anger, her pride, the horrible hurt stinging her heart, the betrayal, she would never forget the time she'd spent with him. And she still didn't love him any less, as foolish as that seemed.

She would also never forget the scene playing out before her at the moment. Chance was standing near the hood of the limo, and Sam was crouched down at his level, preparing to say goodbye. They spoke softly and Andrea strained to hear Sam's parting words. When she couldn't quite make them out, she moved a little closer.

"You must promise me that you will take care of your mother."

"Okay," Chance said reluctantly.

"And you must promise me to take care of Sunny now that she is yours. She's a fine filly, and I trust that you will watch out for her."

Chance frowned. "Will you tell Mama to let me ride her sometime?"

"I'm sure she will allow it once the time is right."

They both remained silent for a moment before Sam laid his palm on Chance's thin shoulder. "Be proud of who you are."

"I am. I'm gonna tell my friends about your country, that it's not just all sand, and that the people are nice and look sort of like me."

Sam attempted a weak smile before his expression turned somber once more. "And most important, you must remember that no matter where he is, or what he is doing, your father will always love you."

Andi looked away before her son could glimpse her tears.

"How do you know that?" Chance asked.

"Because I know you. He would be very proud to have such a strong, wise boy."

Andi forced herself to look at father and son once more, to remember.

After a moment's hesitation, Chance drew Sam into an awkward hug and said, "I love you, Sam, like you're my dad."

Andi's heart completely shattered in that moment, and she wanted desperately to reveal that Sam was, in fact, her son's father. But if Sam had no intention of returning, then it would serve no purpose but to confuse Chance even more. Yet deep down she wondered if on some level Chance did know the truth. Regardless, it would be up to her to provide a happy home, to take care of his needs, and to answer his questions when they happened to come. She also hoped that someday she could love again, find a good father for Chance, although that seemed impossible at the moment.

"Time for breakfast, Little Bit," Tess called from the back door.

Chance headed off at a sprint but stopped and pointed at the limo. "One day I'm gonna get me one of those."

Sam laughed then, a rich deep laugh that Andi would take to memory to add to the rest.

Once Chance was safely inside, Andi approached Sam with tentative steps. "Guess it's time for you to go, huh?"

He surveyed her face a long moment then bracketed her cheeks in his palms. "Take care, Andrea."

"I'm going to be fine, Sam. We're all going to be fine." She said the words with false bravado, determined to act as though she would survive his departure. And she would, even if it took years to get over him.

"I will have my banker send you the information on Chance's trust. I will see that all yours and Chance's financial needs are met."

But not the one need she desired the most, to have him in her life permanently. "I appreciate that."

He softly kissed her lips. "I will forever be sorry for what I have put you through, but I will never regret what we have shared."

"Neither will I," she said sincerely. "And I'll never forget you." Despite the heartache.

He stared at her long and hard. "You must forget, Andrea. You must go forward."

"I could never forget, Sam, and I'm afraid the same holds true for your son."

"The memories eventually will fade for him, and for you."

"If you say so," she said, knowing that years of trying would never erase him from her memory. They never had before. At least Chance was young, resilient, and he had a lifetime ahead of him, even if he wouldn't have the pleasure of knowing his father.

Andi jumped when Rashid started the engine, yet Sam didn't let her go. He lowered his lips to her ear and whispered, "No matter where I am or what I am doing, I will always be thinking of you. I will always hold you close in my heart and love you with all that I am."

Andi swiped furiously at her eyes, now clouded with unwanted tears. "Don't do this to me, Sam. Please go."

He met her gaze. "Before I do go, will you allow me one more kiss?"

Though she knew she shouldn't, she nodded her agreement. His lips were soft and warm and gentle as they claimed hers in a heartfelt kiss, a kiss that expressed the emotions Andi felt so deep inside her soul. Yet it only lasted a brief time before he pulled away.

"Live well, Andrea." With one more soft kiss, he stepped into the limo and closed the door, closed out all that they had known in each other's arms.

After Rashid drove away, Andi stood and watched until she could no longer see the car's taillights. In that moment she made a vow. She would take all the memories and store them away for safekeeping, as Tess had told her she should. Life would go on without Sam, though she might always live with some regrets. But she would have her beloved son, the greatest gift to be had. Sheikh Samir Yaman had given her that much, even if he couldn't give all of himself. For that she would always be grateful.

Sam sat alone in the airport terminal while awaiting the pilot's summons. He watched with new interest the people passing by, yet the families traveling together held his interest most of all. He could see the affection in their faces, the protectiveness of a father tightly gripping his daughter's hand. He viewed the pride in a mother's face when her son said, "Excuse me," as he passed in front of Sam to claim a seat nearby.

A soul-wrenching emptiness flowed through Sam as he acknowledged how much he would lose by not experiencing the same relationship with his son. One day he might have other children, and he would love them equally, but he would always wonder about what might have been had he taken a different path. Had he not been born to royalty.

"The plane is ready, Prince Yaman."

Sam looked up to see Rashid standing over him with his usual detachment. "I am ready." Yet he did not feel ready for this trip. For what awaited him at home. He could only concentrate on what he was leaving behind.

As they traveled down a corridor and onto a tarmac where the private jet awaited them, Rashid began a litany of duties Sam would be facing upon his return. The list continued even after Sam had settled in to his seat for the journey.

"Your father says that you are to report immediately to the palace to sign the agreement."

Not surprising, Sam thought. "I assume my father will be there?"

"Yes, and so will your bride and her father."

Something Sam was already dreading. Since he had decided to call off the arrangement, he preferred to meet with his father alone. "What else?" he asked, although that was quite enough.

"You are to meet with the parliament tomorrow morning to discuss the upcoming election."

"I am aware of that."

"And your father also requests that you speak with your brother."

Sam waved off the male attendant offering a drink. "Which one?"

"Jamal. It seems the young prince is secretly seeing a woman, although her identity has not been revealed."

Good for Jamal. It would please Sam if his brother made his own decision about his life partner. "I refuse to interfere."

Rashid frowned. "This will not sit well with your father."

Neither would refusing to marry Maila. "I understand that, and I will handle it."

Rashid fell silent for a moment then once again took up where he'd left off. "You also have…"

A child that needs you, Sam thought. *A woman who loves you. A place by her side if you so choose. Another home. Another family.*

Sam no longer heard Rashid's voice. He could only hear his son saying how he had longed for Sam to be his father. Andrea saying that she loved him, that she needed him. That she wanted him to stay.

The roar of the plane's engines snapped him back into the present situation. Tightly he gripped the arms of the seat as the plane began to taxi toward the runway.

You must return, echoed in his mind. *You are Samir Yaman, firstborn son of the ruler of Barak.*

Yet another voice overshadowed the other.

You are Chance Samuel Paul Hamilton's father….

He was no longer able to fight the urge to run back to Andrea, back to his son, away from his responsibility, toward a new life. He would only be half a man if he left Andrea behind. An inadequate human being if he disregarded his child.

"Tell the pilot to halt and return to the terminal," he shouted at Rashid as he yanked the seat belt away and stood.

Rashid regarded him with a confused look. "Is there a problem?"

Yes, he had been totally blinded by his royal duties until now.

Duty be damned.

When Sam didn't respond, Rashid gave the order to the pilot. After a moment the plane turned around. When they once again reached the position near the terminal, Sam said, "Open the door." The attendant came to his feet but seemed unable to move. "I said open this door," Sam repeated, more demanding this time.

The man reluctantly complied, and Rashid joined Sam at the opening. "Sheikh Yaman, have you forgotten something?"

Sam looked at him earnestly. "Yes, Rashid, I've forgotten who I am, what I desire as a man, not as a prince. I've forgotten what is important in life."

"Are you saying you will be remaining here?"

"Yes, that is exactly what I am saying. I will remain here with my son and the woman I intend to make my wife."

"But your father—"

"Will more than likely disown me. My mother will cry, yet she has the capacity to understand. I will lose my position as future king but in doing so I will gain some peace. Tell me, Rashid, can you blame me?"

Rashid slowly shook his head. "I suppose I cannot, yet I worry over the fate of our country without your leadership."

Sam braced a hand on Rashid's shoulder. "Do not concern yourself with that. Omar is next in line and he is more adept at leading. He will serve our people well."

Sam started down the steps but halted when Rashid asked, "Will you not be returning?"

Looking back over his shoulder at his faithful companion of seven years, Sam smiled. "That is entirely up to my father's mandate. And my mother's powers of persuasion."

For the first time in many years, Rashid smiled. "I would wager my life on your mother's powers."

Sam hurried down the stairs and headed back toward the terminal at a fast clip, resisting the urge to run. He had not felt such freedom in years, such joy over the prospect of spending his life with Andrea and his child.

If Andrea agreed to welcome him back. If not at first, Sam would make sure she would eventually. In the meantime he had much to do.

"That was the third call in three days." Andi turned from the phone to address her aunt seated at the kitchen table.

"More business, I take it."

"Yes, and that was Adam Cantrell. He has a prospect he wants me to train."

Tess slapped her hands on her thighs and stood. "About time people figured out what a good hand you are."

Andi chewed her bottom lip for a moment. "But how would anyone know?"

"Word of mouth I suppose."

"Or word of Sam."

Tess frowned. "Now why would you think Sam had something to do with this?"

"Because he told me that he wanted to help me establish my career, so this has his mark all over it."

"And what's the big deal if he made a few calls?"

"I want to do this on my own, Tess. I want to build my reputation by myself."

"Speaking of building," Tess said. "You're going to have to add onto the barn if things keep going the way they have been."

Andi had considered that for the past week since Sam left, when she hadn't been thinking about him. "I know, but I need to make some money first."

"It's none of my business, but what about the money Sam put in the bank for you and Chance?"

"I want to save that for Chance's education and any medical expenses."

"If you don't mind me asking, how much money is it, anyway?"

Actually, Andi did mind Tess asking even though she shouldn't. After all, Tess had helped make ends meet by taking in sewing and working part-time at the local grocers. They'd never hidden anything from each other since Chance's birth, so she might as well come clean—at least partially. "Let's just say I've never had that many zeroes in my bank account."

Tess raised a thin brow. "That much, huh?"

"That much."

The roar of a truck pulling up behind the house grabbed their attention. Andi walked to the back door and peered out the window. "I wonder who that is?"

Tess came up behind her. "I dunno, but they sure as heck have a fancy enough truck."

Andi tightened her ponytail and swiped away the straw from her shirt. "I'm a mess. Go see what they want."

Tess shrugged. "If you insist, but if he's cute and

single I'm invitin' him in for something cool to drink.''

''Don't you dare!'' Andi's glare was lost on Tess since she'd already headed out the door.

Keeping her post by the back door, Andi watched curiously as a young man left the truck and handed Tess a small white envelope. The guy looked familiar, but she couldn't place him.

When Tess returned to the kitchen, Andi asked, ''What was that all about?''

Tess offered her the envelope. ''It's for you. That was the Masters kid. Seems he's taken a job nearby.''

Unable to contain her curiosity, Andi tore open the envelope to find a card inside. She read silently until Tess cleared her throat. ''Care to let me in on that?''

''It's an invitation to some kind of reception down the road at the old Leveland Place. It's called Galaxy Farms now.''

''I thought that place was vacant.''

So had Andi. ''It was, but apparently not anymore. Someone must have bought it, although there isn't any name indicating the new owner.''

''Someone rich, no doubt,'' Tess allowed. ''That place is prime horse farm all the way around.''

''No joke.''

Leaning back against the counter, Tess eyed Andi for a moment. ''So?''

''So what?''

''So are you going?''

Andi tossed the card onto the table. ''No.''

''Why not?''

Because she didn't feel like socializing at the moment. Because she'd rather be with her son. ''First of all, it's tonight, and that's very short notice. Second, I don't have anything proper to wear."

"Sure you do. The little black number you wore to the auction. And you need to go because it will be good for business. I'm sure there'll be quite a few bigwigs there for a little practical schmoozing."

She sent Tess a semidirty look. "If you're so gung-ho, then why don't you go schmooze?"

Tess let loose a grating laugh. "Oh, yeah. I'm sure I'd make quite an impression." She pulled a stray piece of hay from Andi's hair. "If you get cleaned up, you'll fit right in. Of course, I'll need to cut up some cucumbers for your eyes so you can get rid of those duffel bags underneath."

Andi's fingertips automatically went to the bags in question. "They're not that bad."

"No, not too bad, but it's obvious to me you haven't been sleeping."

No, she hadn't been, not much. She'd stayed awake at night for hours, but she hadn't been alone. Sam still stalked her mind and even her dreams when she finally did nod off. Several times she'd awakened and reached for him as if she couldn't quite register he was really gone. But he was gone, and she needed to move on with her life as she'd been told time and again by everyone she loved. Although she had no desire to meet a man at the moment, she probably should attend the reception for the business's sake.

"Okay, I'll go." Andi released a long, weary sigh. "But I'm not going to stay long. I want to be here to put Chance to bed."

"I'll put him to bed," Tess stated firmly. "You go and have a good time."

Mingling with money didn't sound like a good time at all. "I'll be home by ten."

"Okay, but I won't wait up just in case the new owner is some high-falutin' unmarried hunk."

"He's probably some overindulged, married drunk."

Tess chuckled as she left the kitchen, and Andi already regretted the decision.

Oh, well. She'd just get lost in the crowd.

There was absolutely no one around.

Maybe everyone had parked behind the massive barn, Andi thought as she pulled up behind the truck stationed in the driveway—the same shiny, extended-cab-with-all-the-options truck Donny Masters had been driving that morning.

Confused and concerned, Andi opened the glove compartment and retrieved the invitation. The date was correct and so was the time, only Andi had decided to arrive a half hour later to shorten the duration. Surely the party hadn't been so dull that everyone had taken their leave early. Or maybe no one had bothered to show. Not likely.

But if that were the case, she'd simply march up to the door, introduce herself to the new owners, maybe have a drink, then be on her merry way.

Andi opened the door and slid from the truck, cursing the tight black dress until her feet hit the ground. How she hated this kind of thing. Hated having to get all fixed up for the sake of some strangers.

When she entered the walkway leading to the front door of the sprawling stone house, a series of tiny lights lining the hedge snapped on. Very impressive, Andi thought as she stepped up onto the front porch.

After taking a deep breath, she pushed the bell, worried when she didn't hear any noise coming from inside. No muffled conversations. Not even any music. More than likely she had been correct in her assumptions that either the guests were gone, or they had never come in the first place. Or it could be the party was in the arena. If so, surely some kind soul would direct her to the festivities.

Soft footfalls signaled someone was about to answer her summons. The door opened to a petite woman—obviously a maid—wearing a neat, black uniform and functional shoes. Andi coveted those shoes at the moment, considering she now wore the hated high heels.

''Welcome,'' the woman said in a voice as soft as her gray eyes. ''We're glad you could join us, Miss Hamilton.''

She knew her name? Obviously the owners had done their homework, whoever they were. Andi decided to let the introductions unfold naturally. ''Thank you. I very much appreciate the invitation.'' And she very much wanted to get this over with and get out of there.

Once inside, Andi studied the lengthy corridor with awe as she followed behind the maid. The polished Italian tile beneath her feet and the ornate chandeliers above her head shouted big bucks. And so did the massive room that she entered, a room filled with fine furniture and tasteful treasures set about the room. A room that was completely deserted otherwise.

"Is the party in the stable?" Andi asked when she saw no sign of food or drink.

The woman only smiled. "He will be with you shortly to answer any questions you might have."

"He who?" Andi asked, totally baffled.

"The master of the house, of course." With that she disappeared.

The maid obviously had vagueness down to a fine art, and this was just a little too weird, in Andi's opinion. Her first instinct told her to get out. Her second involved blatant curiosity.

Although she really didn't sense she was in imminent danger, Andi shot a glance over her shoulder, making sure the path to the door was clear should she have to make a hasty escape. In the meantime she opted to do a little exploring around the area in search of some clue that might indicate who the mysterious "he" might be. Her gaze immediately traveled to the paned window to her right, or more accurately the glittering mobile that hung between the heavy parted curtains.

When she moved closer, she noted the individual crystals were replicas of planets flanked by tiny shimmering stars. Of course, she thought. Galaxy Farms. Very clever.

Unable to resist, Andi reached out and touched the tiny diamond-like stars, setting the mobile in motion. The gentle sway shot beams of color around the immediate area. Absolutely breathtaking, Andi thought. At least the mysterious owner had good taste, whoever he was.

"Are you still so fascinated with the stars, Andrea?"

Ten

Her hand froze midair at the sound of the familiar voice. The deep, endearing voice forever engrained in her memory, in her heart.

Andi shuddered, and a soft keening ring filtered into her ears. No way could this be happening again. Her mind was playing nasty tricks on her, playing havoc with her pulse. She was totally losing it. Sam had left. Gone for good. Forever.

But the reference to the stars…

Unable to turn around, she visually searched the room for some sign that she wasn't totally nuts. Something that would indicate she hadn't completely lost her grip on reality.

Then she saw it.

On a nearby oak table sat a photograph of a beautiful little boy, his adoring mother and dark, handsome father, holding on fast to each other. To any casual observer, they would appear to be any happy family. The family Andi had always wished for, and still did.

She closed her eyes and inhaled deeply, immediately drawing in the familiar, welcome scent of the man whom she'd said goodbye to six days ago. Six long, torture-filled days.

"You did not answer my question, Andrea."

How could she answer his question when she couldn't begin to speak? How could she just stand there and not turn around to verify this was real?

His fingertips skimmed down her arm, and she shivered as if she were totally exposed. In some ways she was, laid emotionally bare once again because of his unexpected return.

"I think I must be dreaming at the moment." Her voice sounded broken, unsure. Hopeful.

His warm breath fanned across her neck and cheek. "This is no dream, Andrea."

Finally she turned around and met his dark, dark eyes. "What are you doing here, Sam?"

He showed a hint of a smile. "I am the new owner."

Too surreal, she thought. Too, too surreal. "You're telling me you've bought this place?" Suddenly it was all too apparent that this was Sam's money and means at work. Sam's way of trying to provide for her without asking. More than likely, he wasn't back to stay. "If you think Chance and I are going to live here, then you—"

He held a fingertip against her lips to silence her. "I do hope you and Chance will decide to live here."

"We already have a place to live, so we'll do no such thing—"

"With me."

"With—" she swallowed hard "—you?"

He slid his knuckles along her jaw in a slow, heavenly rhythm. Andi wanted to close her eyes but feared if she did, he would evaporate into thin air. "Of course we will keep your father's place for Tess and Mr. Parker, and then our son if he so chooses to live there."

Andi blinked once, twice. "I don't understand."

"It is very simple, Andrea. I've realized that my place is here with you and our son."

How long had she waited to hear that? "But what about your duty?"

"My duty lies in my responsibility to you and to Chance. Admittedly it took me some time to realize this, but now that I have, I am hoping you will trust that I intend to stay. Always."

Oh, how Andi wanted to believe him, but it was simply too good to be true. "You'll have divided loyalties, Sam. You'll miss your family."

He circled his arms around her waist and pulled her to him. "You are my family now, Andrea. The rest will work itself out in due time."

"Are you sure, Sam? Are you really sure this is what you want to do? Be with us, day in and day out? No one waiting on you hand and foot, just your average, everyday work?" Another thought crossed her mind. "What would you do here?"

"Other than work very hard to make you happy, I would establish this place as a premiere training facility. With your expertise and my eye for fine stock, we could be very successful.''

Regardless of her caution, Andi couldn't contain her excitement. ''Do you think maybe we could consider breeding?''

Sam grinned. ''I would propose we put that at the top of the list.''

She pinched his side. ''I meant horses.''

''I suppose we could breed those, as well.'' He brushed a chaste kiss across her lips. ''Then you are considering my suggestions?''

How easy it would be to say yes. How very, very easy. After all, wasn't this what she had dreamed about for so long? Sam returning, for good. If it was, in fact, for good.

She moved back, putting some distance between them in order to reclaim her emotional bearings. ''The past few days I've ached to have you back, but I was getting by, the same as I did when you left the first time. But if you ever decided to leave again, I'm not sure if I would survive it the next time.''

''There will be no next time.''

He sounded so sincere, but one very important question still hounded her. ''What about the woman you're supposed to marry?''

''I have spoken with her, and she is very much relieved. It seems she has fallen in love with another man. I am pleased by that fact.''

So was Andi, but she still had more questions. ''And your parents? What do they think about you staying in America?''

He sighed. ''My father has not taken the news well. My mother is somewhat saddened by my decision, yet she told me she knew that when I was born in America, a significant part of my being would always remain in this country.''

Andi realized there were still many things she didn't know about him. "Are you saying you have dual citizenship?''

"Technically, yes. My parents were traveling in the states on a diplomatic mission, visiting with various governors. My mother insisted on accompanying my father despite the fact she was only a few weeks away from delivery. I chose to arrive early on American soil. That is the reason I attended university here, to experience this place, this life.''

"But you've always preferred your father's country.''

"I've always considered it my country, regardless of where I was born. If my father sees fit, I will visit there often, with you and Chance. But I consider my true home to be with you and my son.''

He seemed so convincing, every plan so well thought out. Then why was she still so scared?

As if sensing her reticence, Sam reverently touched her face and searched her eyes. "Trust me, Andrea. I give you my word that I will never leave you again. Never.''

"Do you promise?''

"With all that I am.''

This time Andrea's heart told her that he meant what he'd said. This time she decided to listen.

She opened her arms and smiled through joyful tears. "Welcome home, Sam.''

In a sudden explosion of passion, he kissed her with a fervor that momentarily deprived her of the

ability to breathe, to think. She didn't want to think.
She didn't want to do anything but be with him, to
prove that this was real, the offer of a home and his
love. That he was real.

"Come with me," he whispered softly and took
her hand. She followed as if she had no will of her
own, and that somehow seemed appropriate. Having
strength of will seemed unnecessary. Following Sam
to wherever he might lead her took priority over protest at the moment.

They walked through another long hallway and to
an atrium filled with myriad plants at the rear of the
house. One wall of windows provided a view of a
large yard with a fountain illuminated in blue. Sam
guided her to a plush chaise longue wide enough for
two people. Once they'd settled on the edge, Andi
turned her face to the glass ceiling that revealed a
blanket of stars.

"This is so beautiful, Sam."

"Our very own place under the heavens," he said
in a deep, sensual voice. "A place where we can
make love regardless of the weather."

She regarded him with a smile. "What? And give
up the pond? We can't do that. I'd miss getting eaten
alive by bugs."

He laughed. "That I will not miss at all, but I see
no reason not to visit there for the sake of remembrance." Suddenly serious, he caught her hands and
held them against his pounding heart. "You honor me
by your presence alone, yet I would be more honored
if you would agree to be my wife."

Wife. That one word staggered her soul, set her
mind to reeling. She had always said she had no use

for being anyone's wife, and all along she had been lying to herself. She'd only wanted to be Sam's wife, his life partner. Although she wanted to cry out *yes!* she didn't. Not yet.

Leaning closer, she tickled his ear with the tip of her tongue. "Where's the maid?"

"She took her leave soon after she greeted you, as instructed."

"Good, because I'd really like you to convince me that agreeing to your proposal would be worth my while."

He smiled a beautiful, endearing smile. "I see that you are determined to be obstinate."

She slipped the first button on his nice white shirt that now sported a nice pink lip print on the collar. She'd always wanted to do that, and she planned to do much more. "I'm determined all right, but it has nothing to do with being obstinate, as you will soon find out."

"So be it." He attempted to turn off the nearby floor lamp and she stopped him.

"No," she said adamantly. "No darkness this time, Sam. I want to see you in the light. Every detail."

He reached behind her and slid the zipper down on her dress, his ragged respiration echoing in the room. "Anything you wish, Andrea. Anything at all. You only have to tell me and I will do whatever you ask. Tonight I am yours for the taking. Every night from this point forward, if you so desire."

She desired to sleep with him every night, to wake with him every day, to work with him not only to build a successful business but also to make a secure, loving home for their son. For the remainder of her life.

But tonight she wanted once again to concentrate on showing Sam how much she loved him.

After undressing in a rush, they stretched out on the chaise facing each other. The mutual exploration began with tender touches and ended with fevered caresses. They took turns pleasing each other, committing to memory every detail with hungry hands. Then touches gave way to intimate kisses, leaving no parts of their bodies unexplored.

Feeling bold and brave, Andi nudged Sam onto his back and straddled his thighs, intending to take control over the situation. But awareness of what they needed to do suddenly hit her.

"Do you have any protection, Sam?" she asked.

He clasped her hips in his large hands and inched her forward, very close to dangerous territory. "Will you think I am insane if I ask that we do not consider that tonight?"

"You mean—"

"That I want nothing between us, but only if you are in agreement."

"But I could—"

"Become pregnant again. I know." He cupped the back of her head and brought her forward, then kissed her thoroughly before saying, "Nothing would please me more than to have another child with you. One that I would know from the beginning."

The ultimate proof of his commitment, Andi decided. He would never leave her alone to raise another child, this much she knew. He would never abandon her this time.

Instead of responding with words, she lifted her hips and slowly lowered herself onto him. They kept their gazes locked as well as their bodies as they moved in sync.

It seemed as if they had never made love before, at least to Andi. Every sensation as Sam moved smoothly inside her seemed new, untried. Every passionate word he spoke to her seemed as if she were hearing it for the first time.

Watching his face and knowing her own reflected the same pleasure he enjoyed at this moment only heightened her desire, solidified her love for him.

When neither could hold out any longer, they came apart in each other's arms. Came together in one act of love that would always be beyond compare.

After Andi collapsed against Sam's chest, he told her, "You have yet to give me an answer."

Andi rolled to her side to face him. "I'm thinking we have someone else to ask first."

He raised a dark brow. "Our son?"

"Yes, although I can't imagine he'd put up a fuss once we tell him you're his father."

"I am very much looking forward to that moment."

Andi tucked her head beneath his chin and held him tightly. "In the morning."

"I'd prefer to tell him tonight."

She raised her head and stared in surprise. "Tonight?"

He cupped her breast in his hand. "In a while. I fear that I still have more convincing to do."

Andi wriggled against him, eliciting a groan from Sam. "I believe you do, at that."

* * *

By the time they reached the farm, it was nearing 11:00 p.m. Sam realized that his son could very well be in bed, but he hadn't been able to keep his hands off Andrea, nor had she put up much protest.

Fortunately, the lights still burned bright from the kitchen window as they made their way to the entrance. Once they arrived on the top step, Andrea stopped him from opening the door. "Wait just a sec, okay? I want to have some fun."

He cupped her bottom and pulled her to him, amazed that he was again aroused after such a brief time. Yet he probably shouldn't be amazed at all. Andrea was capable of keeping him in such a state both day and night. "Are you not afraid that Tess might see us?"

She batted at his hand. "Not that kind of fun. I want to play this up with Tess. Boy, will she ever be surprised."

No, she would not, but Sam decided against revealing that fact.

Andrea opened the door, and he glimpsed Tess and Riley Parker seated at the table.

"Hey, you two," Andrea said. "I'd like you to meet the new owner of Galaxy Farms."

Grabbing Sam's hand, she pulled him forward. Tess and Riley did not bother to appear the least bit shocked, as he'd expected.

"Howdy, Sam," Riley said. "Nice night out, ain't it?"

"Real nice," Tess said with a vibrant grin.

Andrea glanced at Sam, then at the couple, before

affording him a stern, suspicious stare. "These two knew about it all along, didn't they?"

"Now don't get your tail in a wringer, Andi," Tess said. "If Sam hadn't told me about his little plan, I wouldn't have tried so hard to convince you to go tonight."

Andrea's mouth opened, no doubt to deliver a protest. "That was not even nice."

"But necessary," Tess stated.

In hopes of calming her down, Sam wrapped his arms around Andrea from behind and pulled her against him. "I will make it up to you in some manner."

"You can bet on that, buster," she muttered, a smile in her voice.

Feeling greatly relieved, he addressed Tess once more. "Has our son already retired?"

Tess nodded toward the hall. "I just tucked him in. I would've told him he might be getting a surprise tonight but I wasn't sure what our girl here was going to do."

Sam was still uncertain since she had yet to give him a solid answer to his marriage proposal. "Do you think he is still awake?"

"Probably so," Riley said. "I imagine he's countin' his fortune. The kid took all my pennies during poker. He's a regular little card shark."

"Even if he's not awake," Tess said, "you need to get him up. He wouldn't want to miss this."

Andrea glanced back at Sam. "She's right, as bad as I hate to admit it."

Sam gestured toward the stairs. "Lead the way."

On the upper floor Andi pushed open the door to

Chance's room. The light from the hall spilled across his son's small body turned toward the wall. Andrea perched on the mattress, snapped on the bedside lamp and gently shook his shoulder. "Chance, sweetie, are you awake?"

"I am now," came a sleepy and somewhat irritable voice. He turned over and rubbed his eyes. "What's up, Mama?"

"You have a visitor."

"Can't be Santa 'cause it's not Christmas." He raised his head and when his gaze met Sam's, a bright smile illuminated his face. He sat up in a rush. "Sam! You came back."

Sam sat on the other side of his son. "Yes, I have returned."

Chance's grin reflected his joy. "I knew you would. Every night I said my prayers and asked for you to come back. I also asked Uncle Paul in case he and God are good friends."

Andrea touched his cheek. "I'm sure they are, honey. Your uncle Paul was always a good friend."

"The best," Sam said in earnest. He felt assured that Paul would very much approve of his love for Andrea and would gladly bless their union, if Andrea acquiesced. He would know in a matter of minutes.

Andrea sent a nervous glance at Sam, then turned her attention to Chance. "We have something very important to tell you, sweetie. Something I hope you will understand."

"What is it?" he asked.

"Well, Sam isn't just a friend. He's your—"

"Father." His knowing smile expanded. "I know,

Mama. I bet Billy Reyna that Sam was my real dad back when we were at camp.''

Sam took a moment to recover his voice. Obviously, they had been wrong to underestimate their son's intuitiveness. ''You have known all along, then?''

He nodded his head with a jerk. ''Sure did. But how come you two waited so long to tell me?''

''It's kind of complicated, Chance,'' Andrea said.

Sam took Chance's hand into his. ''We waited until the moment was right, until I knew for certain that I would be able to stay with you forever.''

Chance's eyes widened. ''Then you are going to stay?''

''Yes, I am. If that is favorable to you and your mother.''

He looked at Andrea. ''It's okay, isn't it, Mama?''

''More than okay. And one more thing.'' She looked lovingly at Sam. ''Your father would like me to marry him so that we can be a family.''

Chance hopped feetfirst onto the bed and released an ear-piercing ''Whoopie!''

Andrea tugged him back to her side. ''I guess that's a yes.''

''Yep, it is.'' Chance frowned. ''As long as you don't kiss and do a lot of that mushy stuff.''

''We'll try to restrain ourselves,'' Andrea said, then laughed. ''At least when you're around.''

Overcome with joy, with love, Sam pulled Chance to his side. ''I am grateful that you understand, my son.''

Awareness dawned in his child's joyous expression. ''Can I call you Daddy now?''

"It would be my fondest wish for you to do so."

Chance pulled him into a voracious hug. "I'm really glad you're back, Daddy."

Sam's heart took flight over that one simple word. "As I am glad to be back."

"Can I go to sleep now?" Chance said through a yawn. "I wanna get up early and call Billy."

Andrea ruffled his hair and kissed his forehead. "Of course. Sweet dreams and see you in the morning."

"Will you be here in the morning, Daddy?"

"Yes, and every morning from this point forward."

Epilogue

From this day forward. How very sweet to have had those words included in their vows, Andi thought as she and Sam arrived hand in hand at the reception in their new home.

She had been so nervous during the wedding, not because of the ceremony itself, just a simple gathering at a nearby wedding chapel. It seemed she'd been waiting a lifetime for the moment when she and Sam were truly together. Her apprehension resulted from the prospect of meeting Sam's family, but only his mother and Sam's brother Omar and his two children came. Now expecting another child, Omar's wife had stayed behind. And Sam's father had refused to join them.

Andi had been shocked to learn that anyone in the family had agreed to come. If only they'd had the opportunity to spend some time together beforehand, then Andi might not be so shaky. But as it had turned out, the royal family hadn't arrived in time for the wedding.

Even though she'd asked Sam a lot of questions about his culture, Andi wasn't sure how she was supposed to act, what she was supposed to say. After all, she was entering a different world. Sam's world. Never before had she shied away from a challenge, but she wanted so badly to please them for Sam's sake.

Sam gave Andi's hand a reassuring squeeze as they paused in the hallway. "You need only be yourself," he said as if he'd read her thoughts.

"I hope that's good enough," Andi said through a forced smile.

He brushed a kiss across her cheek. "Always know that you are the best in my eyes."

Andi took comfort in his words and her anxiety lessened somewhat—until they entered the tent set up outside the atrium. The moment of judgment had arrived, and she sure hoped Sam's family didn't find her lacking. No matter, she decided. She would always have her own little family.

The makeshift ballroom glistened with twinkling white lights crisscrossed on the ceiling, providing the only illumination aside from candles set out on the round tables. Along the perimeter of the tent's walls, banquet tables brimmed with every food imaginable. Main courses on one side, canapés and desserts on the other. At the front of the tent a huge cake draped with lilac flowers flanked a fountain flowing with champagne. And near the chocolate groom's cake sporting a baseball in the center, sat a photo of a smiling young man, the very man who had been responsible for this union.

"Thank you, Paulie," Andi whispered, followed by a smile. Although he wasn't physically present, Andi had no doubt that her brother was looking on from his position among the stars and probably saying, "Poor Sam. Now he has to put up with you."

"It's about time you two got here. I thought you'd stopped somewhere to start the honeymoon." Several people looked up from the feasting over Tess's rather loud greeting.

Blazing heat crept up Andi's face as Sam nudged her forward into the middle of the crowd composed of community leaders, clients and family. Yet Andi couldn't see anyone that she thought to be Sam's mother among the masses, but she had glimpsed her son running about with two beautiful olive-skinned children that she assumed could be Sam's niece and nephew. Chance continued to be totally oblivious to their arrival, and that was okay with Andi. She would visit with him later. Right now she wanted him to get to know his new cousins.

After numerous greetings and good wishes, hugs and happy tidings, Andi followed Sam to the head table and accepted the champagne he offered her. From the corner of her eye, Andi noted a tall, elegant woman wearing a long navy gown, her hair pulled back into a neat chignon. She had no doubt this was Sam's mother. The resemblance was truly remarkable. Nearby stood a man in traditional Arab dress, and Andi assumed this to be Sam's brother.

Sam nudged her forward. "Come. I will introduce you."

After gulping a long drink, Andi allowed Sam to take her elbow and guide her toward the pair. Her heart drummed in her chest with every footstep.

Once they arrived at the place where the strangers now stood, Sam said, "It is my honor to present my wife, Andrea. Andrea, my mother, Amina, and my brother Omar."

Omar gave her a courteous nod, looking somewhat aloof and very much like Sam, aside from a neatly trimmed goatee. On the other hand, Sam's mother smiled, catching Andi off guard. "My son has done very well, I see," she said. "We are very happy to welcome you into the family, Andrea." Her voice was kind, sophisticated and laced with a lyrical accent.

Andi held out her hand that Amina took without hesitation. "I am very happy to be in the family."

Omar's serious expression suddenly melted into a dimpled grin. "I welcome you as well, Andrea. You are to be commended for taming my rogue brother."

Sam looked totally incensed. "You are one to talk, Omar. Had it not been for Sadiiqa's kindness in accepting you as her husband, I have no doubt you would still be jet-setting throughout Europe, bedding every woman—"

"Enough," Amina stated firmly with the hint of another smile. "Do you both wish to have Andrea believe I have raised two hellions?" She laid a dramatic hand on her heart. "Forgive them, Andrea. No matter how many years pass, they are still inclined to behave like young boys."

Andi laughed. "I understand completely." And she did. Years before, Sam and Paul had acted much the same. How wonderful to see it happening again.

Omar gestured across the room. "I believe I must tend to my children since I see that Jassim is unhappy. No doubt a minor crisis has arisen between him and his sister."

"No doubt your daughter has only defended herself," Amina said. "She is as strong as any boy, I am proud to say."

"Obviously you have taught her well, Mother," Sam said in a mock-serious tone. "Omar, would you tell Chance that his mother has summoned him?"

Omar nodded again. "Most certainly."

After Omar took his leave, Amina turned to Andi once more. "I have enjoyed visiting with your aunt. She has shared with me the finer points of Southern cooking, although I am still not certain about the collard greens."

Leave it to Tess to bridge the cultural gap with country cuisine. "If I were you, I wouldn't worry about it. They're not exactly my favorite."

Taking Andi by both hands, Amina stepped back and looked her up and down. "Your dress is simply exquisite."

Andi sneaked a quick glance over her sleeveless satin bridal gown. "It's simple, like me."

Amina released Andi's hands and gently patted her cheek. "There is much beauty in simplicity. One only has to look at the heavens to realize this. The stars are beautiful in their simplicity.''

In that moment Andi felt a true affinity with Sam's mother. Maybe she might fit in after all. "I couldn't agree more." Sam only smiled.

Amina's features turned solemn as she regarded her son. "Samir, I will not attempt to apologize for your father's absence. I will ask you to be patient." She addressed Andi once more. "He is a somewhat stubborn man, yet he truly loves his family. He sees this as a loss of his child."

"It does not have to be that way, Mother," Sam said adamantly.

She laid a slender hand on Sam's arm. "I realize this, my beloved son, and he will realize the same eventually. I do hope you can make amends at your brother's wedding in three months' time. You will consider attending?"

Sam frowned. "What wedding?"

"Jamal's wedding."

Rubbing his jaw, Sam smiled. "Ah, so I assume the mystery woman has been revealed."

Amina glanced away and wrung her hands. "Yes, she has, and I hope it will please you."

"Who is this woman?"

"Maila."

Andi stifled a gasp and Sam looked no less shocked and somewhat angry. "So Father has replaced me with Jamal. How convenient."

"You are very wrong, Samir," Amina scolded. "Jamal and Maila are together at their own insistence, without the benefit of an arrangement. It is a love match in every sense of the word.''

''I am glad,'' Sam said sincerely.

And so was Andi. She could greatly appreciate two people falling in love. Sometimes destiny just couldn't be denied.

''Have you told Father about Chance?'' Sam asked.

Andi had wondered if Amina knew that Sam was Chance's father but hadn't asked. She decided that Sam would be the best judge of how to handle that news. Obviously he had handled it.

''I believe it best that he meet his grandson in person,'' Amina said. ''I, too, am waiting for an official introduction. And it seems that moment has arrived.''

In that instant Chance rushed to Andi and grabbed her around the waist. ''That man said you want me, Mama, but I'm playing with these kids from Daddy's country and we're having fun. Can I go back now?''

''Not yet,'' Andi said as she turned Chance around to face Amina. ''First, there's someone we'd like you to meet.''

Amina knelt on Chance's level. ''Chance, I am your *jadda*.''

He wrinkled his nose, a sure sign of his confusion. ''My what?''

''Your grandmother,'' Sam stated. ''My mother.''

Looking as if they'd handed him the world in a basket, Chance grinned. ''For real? I don't have one of those.''

Amina drew him into a quick, heartfelt hug. ''You most certainly have one now, little one.''

Andi half expected Chance to protest another relative referring to him as "little," but he only continued to smile.

"Do you live in my daddy's country?" he asked.

"Yes, I do, and I hope you will come visit one day." She touched his face with maternal reverence. "The children with whom you are playing are your cousins, and their father is your uncle Omar."

Chance glanced back at Andi. "Like Uncle Paul?"

"Yes," she said. "Like Uncle Paul."

"Cool." He looked back at the place where Omar stood with his son and daughter. "Can I go play with my cousins now? I want to take them to the barn to see Sunny."

"Okay, but make sure you go with an adult," Andi said.

"I will go," Amina offered. "But first, who is this Sunny?"

"My horse," Chance said, taking Amina by the hand. "You're going to love her, Grandma. Can I call you Grandma?"

"Oh, most certainly. Did you know you look very much like your father did when…"

As she watched Amina drape her arm around Chance's shoulder, as she observed the children jumping up and down with excitement as they headed away, Andi realized there wasn't so much difference after all. Family was family, regardless of cultural diversity. That diversity made the moments all the more special. After all, love knew no real boundaries.

"Would you care to escape with me for a moment?" Sam whispered.

"I suppose I could for a while," she said. "But

eventually we're going to have to cut that mammoth cake.''

"The cake can wait a few more moments. At present I would like to be alone with my bride.''

Andi followed Sam from the tent and back into the atrium. Once there he turned her into his arms and kissed her, but good—very, very good.

Just when Andi considered saying, To heck with the cake, let's go upstairs, Sam broke the kiss.

"I am losing my control," he said, winded.

"Do you hear me objecting?"

"No, but I do believe I heard you moan."

She playfully slapped at his hand that had somehow landed on her bottom. "I'm sure it won't be the last time tonight."

"I do wish you had allowed me to take you somewhere for a honeymoon," he said.

"You know we can't do that right now. We have to be here for Riley and Tess's wedding next week. I need to get Sunny well underway, not to mention the other ten horses in the barn. Besides, we have a nice big bed upstairs with a huge whirlpool tub in the bathroom. Who could ask for more?"

"I suppose you are right," he said, looking too, too somber. "And as it now stands, we should probably be prudent with our funds. I have spent a great deal on this place, and until we begin to see a profit, we will have to rely on what I have left of my own investments since my father has withdrawn his support."

Andi touched his face. "We have so much now, Sam. We're going to do fine. And I know how badly you hurt over your father's attitude, but I'm inclined to believe your mother. He'll come around.''

''I do most admire your optimism, but I also know my father very well.''

''And I never believed we would be together, either.''

Sam caught her hands and kissed each palm. ''Nor did I.''

Andi shrugged. ''Besides, once we see him face-to-face, once he sees how much we love each other, he'll have to believe it was meant to be. And I'm sure he'll be very taken with his charming grandson.''

''On the topic of children, will there be another child in our near future?''

''I hope so,'' Andi said with a smile. ''But not this time.''

''Then you are not—''

''Pregnant. No. At first I was disappointed, then I decided that it will happen when the time is right.'' She pulled him close and couldn't resist executing a little wriggle against one of Sam's finer qualities. ''I'm sure you'll eventually get the job done, and quite sufficiently.''

He tugged at the collar of his tuxedo. ''I believe we shall have a lengthy practice tonight.''

''I'm willing to give for the cause.''

Sam sighed. ''I wish that I could give you everything your heart desires.''

Andi rested her cheek against his chest, against his strong heart. ''You *have* given me everything, Sam. A wonderful home. A family. A beautiful child. But you know what?''

Andi looked into the eyes of her husband and no longer saw any real mystery there. She only saw his love, bold and beautiful beneath the stars that shone above them.

"The best gift you have given me, the greatest gift anyone could ever receive, is your love. Without that, all the gold in the world would mean nothing."

Softly he kissed her lips. "How very true, Andrea. How very, very true."

*   *   *   *   *

*If you enjoyed THE SHEIKH'S BIDDING,
you will love Kristi Gold's next book:
RENEGADE MILLIONAIRE
Available March 2003.
Don't miss it!*